Dear Reader,

As a single woman, I know that trying to meet Mr. Right can be exasperating—and incredibly exciting. Some say love happens when you least expect it. And that's what Yours Truly is all about. A new line of charming, clever love stories in which men and women meet—not only when they least expect to, in *ways* they least expect to.

Take, for example, *Wanted: Perfect Partner* by Debbie Macomber, one of our two terrific launch titles. In this warm, witty novel, a divorced mom meets the man of her dreams through a personal ad that *she* never placed. And in Lori Herter's hip, humorous *Listen Up, Lover,* an alluring written announcement leads California's most confirmed bachelor to walk his very cold feet down the aisle.

You see, Yours Truly characters meet unexpectedly through forms of written communication, such as personal ads, love notes from secret admirers, wedding invitations—even license plates! If you've ever met someone special through written communication, send me a *brief* account (50 words) of your real-life Yours Truly romance. If you include permission for me to edit and print your story, you might see it on a special page in the months to come!

Each month, look for two Yours Truly titles—entertaining, engaging romance novels about meeting, dating... marrying Mr. Right.

Yours truly,

Melissa Senate

Editor

Please address questions and book requests to:
Silhouette Reader Service
U.S.: 3010 Walden Ave., P.O. Box 1325, Buffalo, NY 14269
Canadian: P.O. Box 609, Fort Erie, Ont. L2A 5X3

DEBBIE MACOMBER

Wanted: Perfect Partner

SILHOUETTE YOURS TRULY™

Published by Silhouette Books
America's Publisher of Contemporary Romance

SILHOUETTE BOOKS

ISBN 0-373-52001-8

WANTED: PERFECT PARTNER

About the author

DEBBIE MACOMBER has always enjoyed telling stories, first to baby-sitting clients, and then to her own children. An avid reader, she wanted to share her stories with a wider audience. Debbie's first book was published by Silhouette in 1983, and she was off and running. Now, more than fifty books later, her titles consistently hit number one on the Waldenbooks Bestseller list, and she is a two-time winner of the B. Dalton Bestseller Award.

When asked how she got the idea for *Wanted: Perfect Partner*, Debbie said, "I know what you're thinking and you're *wrong*. I've never answered a personal ad. Not that I haven't been tempted. Not for myself, mind you, but on behalf of my unmarried daughter, Jody. I've found the perfect man for her a dozen or more times, but that daughter of mine is an independent cuss and prefers to find her own husband. And so I've been left to imagine what would happen if I were to 'arrange something' for Jody, the way Lindsey Remington does for her mother."

In addition to Silhouette books, Debbie also writes mainstream novels. She's always delighted to hear from her readers and can be reached at: P.O. Box 1458, Port Orchard, WA 98366.

Prologue

◀—▶

"Is our ad there?" Fifteen-year-old Lindsey Remington whispered to her best friend. She glanced nervously toward her bedroom door, and held her breath. Her biggest fear was that her mother would find her and Brenda scanning the Dateline section of the Wednesday newspaper and discover what they'd done.

Okay, so it was a bit underhanded to write an ad on her mother's behalf, but it was clear to Lindsey that her parent needed help.

It wasn't as if Lindsey could pull a potential husband out of a top hat without a bit of assistance. So she wrote an ad, with her best friend advising her.

"Here," Brenda said excitedly, pointing to the middle of the printed page. "It's here. Oh, my goodness. It's really here, just the way we wrote it."

Lindsey's eyes found the spot on the printed page. She read aloud:

"Wanted: Perfect partner. Looks like a beauty queen, cooks like a mom, kisses like a woman in love. Dating-shy divorcée seeks a man with marriage on his mind. Box 1234.''

"It sounds even better in print," Brenda said.

"Do you think anyone will actually respond?" Lindsey asked.

"I bet we get lots of letters."

"I still think we should have said she has kisses that taste better than chocolate."

"It didn't fit. Remember?" The two had worked long and hard over the wording of the ad. Lindsey had insisted on describing her mother as stunning, and Brenda was afraid it might not fit in with the truth-in-advertising rules.

All right, so her mother wasn't Miss World material, but she was very pretty. Or she could be, with a little help from the advice offered in several magazines Lindsey had been reading lately. Luckily she had a daughter who knew the ropes.

"Don't worry, Lindy," Brenda said with a romantic sigh. "This is the best thing you could ever have done for your mother."

Lindsey hoped her mother appreciated her efforts. "Just remember this guy has to be perfect. We'll need to be careful who we pick."

"Not a problem. If we don't like the sound of one guy, then we'll choose someone else," Brenda said, as if it they were destined to have tons of applicants. "That's the beauty of our plan. We'll screen all the applicants before your mother has a chance to date them. How many teenagers get to choose their stepfathers in advance? Not many, I bet."

Lindsey returned her attention to the ad and gnawed on the corner of her lip. She was experiencing a twinge of pride along with a mild onset of guilt.

Her mother wasn't going to like this. When Meg first learned what she and Brenda had done, she'd probably get all bent out of shape.

As for the ad, Lindsey was downright proud of that. If she were a man inclined to read the Dateline section, the ad would intrigue her.

"Some men will want to write simply because your mom's pretty, but it's the part about her being a good cook that will interest a whole lot more," Brenda assured her. "My grandma claims Grandpa married her because of the way she made German potato salad. Can you believe it?"

Brenda brought up a good point. "How will we know if a man is marrying her for her looks or her meat loaf?"

"We won't," Brenda said, "but by then we'll be out of the picture. Your mother will be on her own."

Lindsey wished she knew more about men. Unfortunately her experience with the opposite sex was limited. She'd only gone on two real dates and both times had been to school dances. And her mother had been a chaperone both times.

"The day will come when Mom will appreciate the sacrifice we made on her behalf," Lindsey said. "She was the one who always claimed how important it was to go after one's dreams. She needs a man. She just doesn't know it yet."

"All she needs is a little help from the two of us."

"And she's got it," Lindsey said, smiling broadly.

1

Those girls were up to something. Meg Remington peeked in her fifteen-year-old daughter's bedroom to discover Lindsey and her best friend, Brenda, crouched on the floor beside the bed. Their knees were scrunched up under their noses and they were heatedly debating something in whispers.

Meg cleared her throat and instantly both girls clammed up tighter than a seal on a pint-size canning jar.

"Hi, Mom," Lindsey said, her bright blue eyes flashing.

Meg knew the look and it generally spelled trouble. "What are you two doing?"

"Nothing."

"Nothing," Brenda echoed, with angelic innocence.

Meg crossed her arms and leaned her shoulder against the doorjamb. She had all the time in the world, and she wanted them to know that. "Tell me why I don't believe that. You two have got the look."

"The look?" Lindsey repeated, and turned to lock gazes with Brenda.

"Yeah. It's one every mother recognizes. You're up to something, and I want to know what it is." She crossed her ankles, indicating that she would make herself comfortable until they were ready to let her in on their little secret. She could wait them out if need be.

"All right, if you must know," Lindsey said with a shrug of defeat. She leapt to her feet and Brenda followed suit. "But we haven't finished planning everything yet."

"I must know." It amazed Meg how beautiful her daughter had gotten to be over the past couple of years. She had gone from the gangly, awkward, big-teeth stage to looking like a princess almost overnight. Meg's ex-husband, Dave, had commented on the changes in Lindsey when she'd flown from Seattle to Los Angeles to visit over spring break. Their little girl was growing up.

"We've been doing some heavy-duty planning," Brenda explained, "and it got fairly involved."

"And exactly what is it the two of you are working on so hard? I haven't seen hide nor hair from you all evening." Generally, when Brenda spent the night, which was at least one night of every weekend, the two were up until all hours playing music, watching television or rented videos. The house had been suspiciously quiet all evening. Come to think of it, they'd been spending a lot of time in Lindsey's bedroom of late. Far too much time. The teens were up to something, and it was time to find out exactly what it was.

Once more the girls found it necessary to study each other before answering.

"You tell her," Brenda urged, "she's your mother."

"I know," Lindsey agreed, and brushed the long strands of hair from her shoulder, "but it might be a little easier coming from you."

"Lindsey?" Meg admitted to being downright curious now.

"You'd better sit down, Mom." Lindsey took Meg by the hand and led her to the bed.

Meg sat on the edge of the mattress. Both teenagers stood in front of her and seemed to be waiting for the other one to speak first.

"You're really a very attractive woman," Lindsey began.

Meg frowned. This sounded like a setup to her, and the best way to handle that was to get straight to the issue. "You need money? How much, and for what?"

With a flair for the dramatic, Lindsey rolled her eyes. "I don't need any money. I meant what I said— you're a beautiful woman."

"It's true," Brenda piped in. "And you're only thirty-four."

"I am?" Meg needed to think about that. Her age wasn't something she dwelled on often. "Yeah, I guess I am."

"You're in the prime of your life."

"I wouldn't go so far..."

"You've still got it, Mrs. Remington," Brenda cut in, with all the emotion of someone making a plea for starving orphans. "You're young and pretty and single, and you've got it." Her fist flew through the air and punctuated the comment.

"Got it?" Meg was beginning to feel like a parrot repeating everything that was said to her.

"You're not in bad shape, either," Lindsey commented, holding her chin in one hand.

Meg sucked in her stomach and was beginning to feel downright pleased with her daughter and Brenda's assessment of her. It seemed rare indeed to have a daughter who was attuned to her mother's finer qualities. Meg had been truly blessed.

"Of course you could look worlds better if you lost ten pounds."

Ten pounds. Meg breathed again and her stomach pouched out. Those ten pounds had made their appearance when Meg was pregnant with Lindsey nearly sixteen years earlier. She was downright proud of having maintained that weight for all these years.

"Ten pounds isn't all that much to lose," Brenda said confidently, as if all Meg really needed was an industrial-size jar of thigh cream.

"It won't be difficult—especially with the two of us helping you."

Meg stared into two eager, expectant faces. "Why is it so all-fired important that I lose ten pounds? I happen to like the way I look."

"There's more."

Meg glanced from one girl to the next. "More? What is that supposed to mean?"

"You need to be physically fit. Think about it, Mom. When was the last time you ran an eight-minute mile?"

Meg didn't need to mull that over at all—she already knew the answer. "Never." Running had never been her thing. She jogged around the track during high school, but only because it was required of her. The lowest grade she'd ever received had been in physical education.

"See," Lindsey said to Brenda.

"We'll help her," Brenda answered, from the side of her mouth. "But we're going to have to start soon."

Lindsey crossed her arms and carefully scrutinized Meg. "About your clothes, Mom."

"My clothes?" Meg cried, still amazed that her daughter thought it was important that she run an eight-minute mile. She owned a bookstore, for heaven's sake. In the eight years since she had bought out Mr. Olsen, not once had she been required to run for anything.

"I want to know what's going on here," Meg said. She had the right. Every time they opened their mouths, the girls confused her more.

"I promise we'll answer all your questions in a minute," Brenda explained. "Please be patient."

Lindsey's hand hadn't left the side of her face. Jack Benny would have been proud of the wonderful imitation she did of him. "Mom, I don't mean to be rude or anything, but when it comes to your choice of clothes, you need help."

"Help?" And to think Meg had been dressing on her own for the past thirty-odd years and no one had bothered to tell her, until now, what a poor job she'd done of it.

"I'm here to see you don't wear polyester ever again," Lindsey said, as though pledging her life to a crusade.

"So you two are official members of the fashion police now?" Meg asked. Apparently they'd issued an APB out on her!

Lindsey and Brenda giggled.

"That's what it sounds like."

"We're here to help you," Brenda said in loving tones.

"We're here to keep you from committing those FNs."

"FNs?" Meg was lost.

"Fashion no-no's."

Meg should have known. "Do you two mind telling me what this little heart-to-heart talk is all about?"

"You, Mom," Lindsey said, in a voice that suggested the answer should have been obvious.

"Why now? Why me?"

"Why not?" Lindsey asked.

Meg started to get up off the end of the bed, but Lindsey directed her back onto the mattress. "We aren't finished yet. We're just now getting to the good part."

"Honey, I appreciate what you're doing, but..."

"Sit down, Mom," Lindsey instructed in stern tones. "I haven't told you the most important part yet."

Meg held up both hands. "You mean there's more?"

"We've already established that you're relatively young," Brenda said.

Lindsey smiled sweetly—the kind of smile a spider gives a fly inviting it onto its web, Meg suspected. "You could still have more children if you wanted...."

"Now wait a minute. . . ." Meg cried.

"What we're really saying is that you're young and attractive."

"Or I could be," Meg amended, "with a little assistance from the two of you."

"But not all that much help," Brenda added sympathetically. "We just want to get you started on the right track."

"I see," Meg muttered.

"Together," Lindsey said, slipping her arm around Brenda's waist, and beaming a proud smile, "we're here to find you a husband."

"A husband." Meg's feet went out from under her and she slipped off the edge of the mattress and landed with a solid whack on the carpet.

Lindsey and Brenda each grabbed one arm and helped her off the floor. "Are you all right?" Lindsey asked, sounding genuinely concerned.

"You should have been more subtle," Brenda insisted accusingly. "There was no need to blurt it out like that."

Meg rubbed her bruised posterior, and sat back down on the bed. "What in the name of heaven makes either of you think I want a husband?" she demanded, flustered to the point of near hysteria. She'd already been through one bad marriage, and she wasn't eager to repeat the experience.

"When was the last time you went out on a date?" Lindsey asked, her question oozing with righteousness.

The kid could make a career out of evangelism if she continued in this vein, Meg decided.

"I don't remember," she snapped. "What does it matter, anyway?"

"Mother, it's clear to me you aren't thinking about the future."

"The future?" The parrot had returned.

"Do you realize that in three short years I'll be in college?"

"Three years," Meg repeated. "No-o I guess I hadn't given the matter much thought." Although at the moment sending her daughter away for four long years sounded downright appealing.

"You'll be all alone."

"Alone isn't such a bad thing," Meg assured them.

"At thirty-seven it is," Lindsey said, with all the drama of a soap-opera star. "I'll worry myself sick about you," she continued, undaunted.

"She will," Brenda confirmed, nodding twice, profoundly.

It was a good thing Meg was sitting down, because she wasn't sure her legs would have supported her much longer had she been upright.

"If for no other reason," Lindsey said, "what could dating again hurt?"

"Honey, has it ever occurred to you that I'm happy with my life just the way it is?"

"No," Lindsey returned. "You aren't happy. You're content with letting life pass you by. It's time to stop dreaming and take action. I don't know what went wrong between you and Dad. I was too young to know what was going on when you divorced, but whatever it was must have been traumatic. To the best of my knowledge, you haven't had a relationship since.''

"It was a friendly divorce." In fact, Meg got along with Dave better now than she had when they were married.

Brenda shook her head knowingly. "There's no such thing as a friendly divorce. My dad's an attorney and he should know."

"I don't want to talk about the divorce," Meg said in her sternest voice. "It happened a long time ago and dragging it through the mud now isn't going to help anyone."

"It might help you," Lindsey said, her eyes an intense blue and as serious as Meg could ever remember seeing them. "But I can understand your reluctance. Besides," she said, and a bright smile transformed her face, "you're going to get all the help you need from Brenda and me."

"That's what I was afraid of," Meg said softly. She stood and started toward the door.

"Your diet starts first thing in the morning," Lindsey called after her.

"And your exercise regime," Brenda added. "You haven't got a thing to worry about, Mrs. Remington. We're going to hook you a man before you know it."

Meg closed her eyes. If thirty-four was so young, why didn't she have the energy to stand up to these two? She wasn't going on any diet, nor was she interested in exercising.

As for having Lindsey scrutinizing her wardrobe... Why that was pure nonsense, and Meg intended to tell both her daughter and Brenda exactly that.

She would, too, first thing in the morning.

Meg soon learned exactly how serious Lindsey and Brenda were over the matter of finding her a husband. She woke Saturday morning to the sound of a workout video playing loudly from the television.

One side of her face was flattened against the mattress and her arm hung over the side of the bed, her fingertips dangling an inch or so above the carpet.

"You ready, Mrs. Remington?" Brenda called from the doorway of Meg's bedroom.

She tried to ignore the teenager, but that didn't work.

"You ready?" Brenda called a second time. From the sounds the girl made, she seemed to be jogging in place. "You don't need to worry, we'll go nice and slow in the beginning."

"I'm not doing anything without speaking to my attorney first," Meg assured her. She stuck out her arm and blindly searched for her telephone.

"Cute, Mom, real cute, but it isn't going to work." Lindsey walked into the bedroom and set a coffee mug down on the nightstand.

"Bless you, my child," Meg said, thinking it was coffee. She struggled into a sitting position before she realized caffeine didn't have anything to do with what Lindsey had brought her. "What's this?" she barked.

"It's a protein supplement. The lady at the health food store highly recommends it for toning skin for women over thirty."

"Are you sure you're supposed to drink it?" Meg asked.

Lindsey and Brenda looked at each other blankly.

"I better check the instructions again," Lindsey said and carried it away.

"Don't worry, Mrs. Remington, we'll have you whipped into shape in no time whatsoever."

"Coffee," she pleaded. She couldn't be expected to do battle without being fortified with caffeine. Surely the Geneva Convention listed something for the protection of unsuspecting mothers.

"You can have your coffee," Brenda promised her, "but first..."

Meg didn't bother to listen to the rest. She slithered back under the covers and protected her head with a pillow. Although the pillow did block out some of the noise, she had no trouble hearing the girls. They weren't accepting defeat lightly. They underwent a lively discussion about the pros and cons of allowing Meg to drink coffee. She had news for these two dictators. Meg would like to see either one try to stand between her and her first cup of coffee.

The conversation swayed to the topic of the divorce and Brenda seemed to believe there were severe psychological hang-ups that had prevented Meg from pursuing another relationship.

It was all Meg could do to keep from shoving the pillow aside and putting in her two cents' worth. What she should have done was order them from the bedroom, but frankly she was curious to hear what they had to say.

Her divorce hadn't been as bad as all that. She and Dave had made the mistake of marrying too young. Meg had barely been nineteen when she'd given birth to Lindsey, and Dave was fresh out of college. In the five years of their marriage there hadn't been any ugly fights or bitter disagreements. Maybe it would have helped matters if there had been.

By the time Lindsey was four, Dave had announced he didn't love Meg any more and he wanted a divorce. It shouldn't have come as a surprise, but it did—and it hurt. Meg knew without having to ask that he'd found someone else.

She was right.

For a long time after the divorce was final, Meg tried to convince herself her failed marriage didn't matter. She and her husband parted on friendly terms. For Lindsey's sake, Meg had made sure they maintained an amicable relationship.

Dave had deeply hurt her, and Meg had denied that pain far too long. Afterward, her energy had been steered in positive ways. It was over now, no big deal, and she was perfectly content with her life.

Between the bookstore and a fifteen-year-old daughter, Meg had left little time for seeking out new relationships. The first few years following the divorce there had been a number of opportunities to become involved again. She hadn't. At the time, Meg simply wasn't interested, and as the years progressed she stopped thinking about it.

"Mother, would you please get out of this bed," Lindsey said, standing over her. Then in enticing tones, she added, "I have coffee."

"You tricked me before."

"This time it's real coffee. The other stuff, well, I apologize about that. I guess I misunderstood the lady at the health food store. You were right. According to the directions you're supposed to use it in the bath, not drink it. Sorry about that."

Meg could see it wasn't going to do the least bit of good to hide her face under a pillow. "I can't buy my way out of this?" she asked, hating herself for being so weak.

"Nope."

"You'll feel much better after you exercise," Brenda promised her. "Really, you will."

Meg didn't feel any such thing. An hour later she couldn't move without some part of her anatomy protesting.

"You did great, Mrs. Remington," Brenda praised.

Meg limped into her kitchen and slowly lowered herself into a chair. Who would have believed a little thing like a workout video, followed by a short—this was the term the girls used—one-mile run would reduce her to this. In the past hour she'd been poked, prodded, pushed and punished.

"I've got your meals all planned out for you," Lindsey informed her. She opened the refrigerator door and brought a sandwich bag. She held it up for Meg's inspection. "This is your lunch."

Meg would have asked her about the meager contents if she'd had the breath to do so. All she could see was one radish, a square of cheese, low fat, she presumed, and a small bunch of seedless grapes.

"Don't have anything more than the nonfat yogurt for breakfast, okay?"

Weak as she was, Meg nodded, rather than dredge up the necessary energy to argue.

"Are you going to tell her about dinner?" Brenda prodded.

"Oh, right. Listen, Mom, you've been a real trooper about this and we thought we should reward you. Tonight for dinner you can have a baked potato."

She managed a weak smile. Visions of butter and sour cream waltzed through her head.

"With fresh grilled swordfish."

"You like fish don't you, Mrs. Remington?"

Meg nodded. At this point she would have agreed to anything just to get the girls out of the kitchen, so she could recover enough to cook herself a decent breakfast.

"Brenda and I are going shopping," Lindsey announced, as if this was of profound importance. "We're going to pick out a whole new wardrobe for you, Mom."

"It's the craziest thing," Meg told her best friend, Lois Harris, that same afternoon. The two were unpacking boxes of books in the back room. "All of a sudden, Lindsey announces she wants me to remarry."

"Really?"

Lois found this far too humorous to suit Meg. "But she wants me to lose ten pounds and run an eight-minute mile first."

"So that's what that was all about," Lois muttered, shuffling paperbacks from the thick cardboard box the publishers used for shipping and onto a cart.

"What?"

"Lindsey was in the store one day two weeks or so ago looking for a book that explained fat grams."

"I'm allowed thirty fat grams a day," Meg informed her. Not that her fifteen-year-old daughter was going to dictate to her what she did and didn't eat.

"I hope Lindsey doesn't find out about that submarine sandwich you ordered for lunch."

"I couldn't help it," Meg said defending herself. "I haven't been that hungry in years. I don't think anyone bothered to tell Lindsey and Brenda that one of the effects of a hard aerobic workout is a voracious appetite."

"What was that phone call about earlier?" Lois wanted to know.

Meg frowned as she shuffled books onto the cart. "Lindsey wanted my credit card number for a slinky black dress with sequins around the scooped neckline and fringe at the hem." She couldn't believe it even now. Lindsey had sounded rapturous over the dress, describing it in detail, especially the deep cuts up both sides that would reveal plenty of thigh. "She claimed she found it on sale for a song...a deal too good to pass up."

"What would Lindsey want with a slinky black dress like that?"

"She wanted it for me," Meg said, under her breath.

"You?"

"Apparently once I fit the proper mold, they plan to dress me up and escort me around town."

Lois laughed.

"I'm beginning to think you might not be such a good friend after all," Meg told her employee. "I expected sympathy and advice, not laughter."

"I'm sorry, Meg, really I am."

She sounded far more amused than she did sorry.

Meg cast her friend a disgruntled look. "You know what your problem is, don't you?"

"Yes," Lois was quick to tell her. "I'm married, with college-age children. I don't have to put up with any of this nonsense and you do. Wait, my dear, until Lindsey gets her driver's license. Then you'll know what real fear is."

"One disaster at a time, thank you." Meg plopped herself down on the stool and reached for her coffee cup. "I don't mind telling you I'm worried."

"Really?" Lois straightened and reached for her cup, refilling it from the freshly brewed pot. "It's a stage Lindsey's going through. Trust me, it'll pass in time."

"Lindsey claims she's worried that I'll be lonely when she leaves for college, which she reminded me is in three short years."

"Will you be?"

Meg had to think about the answer to that. "I don't know. I suppose that in some ways I will be. The house will feel empty without her." The two weeks Lindsey spent with her father every year seemed interminable. Meg wandered around the house like a lost puppy.

"Why not get involved in another relationship?" Lois asked.

"With who?" was Meg's first question. "I don't know any single men."

"Sure you do," Lois countered. "There's Ed, the insurance salesman two doors down from the store."

"Ed's single?" She rather liked Ed. He was the decent sort, but she'd never thought of him in terms of dating. Frankly, she didn't think they'd gel as a couple.

"The fact you didn't know Ed was single says a lot. You've got to keep your eyes and ears open."

"Who else?"

"Buck's divorced."

Buck was a regular customer, and for no reason she could understand Meg had never much cared for him. "I wouldn't date Buck."

"I didn't say you had to date him, I was just saying he was single."

Meg couldn't see herself kissing either man. "Anyone else?"

"There are lots of men out there."

"Oh, really, and I'm blind?"

"Yes," Lois countered. "If you want the truth, I don't think Lindsey's got such a bad idea. True, she may be going about it the wrong way, but it wouldn't hurt you to test the waters. You might be surprised at what you find."

Meg couldn't believe what she was hearing. She had expected support from her best friend, and instead Lois had turned into another Tokyo Rose.

By the time Meg had closed up the bookstore and headed home, she was exhausted. So much for all the claims about exercise filling one with energy.

"Lindsey," she called out, "are you home?"

"I'm in my room," came the muffled reply from the bedroom at the top of the stairs.

Something she couldn't put her finger on prompted Meg to make the long, painful trek up the stairway to her daughter's bedroom. She knocked once and opened the door to discover Lindsey and Brenda sitting on top of the bed, leafing through a stack of letters.

Lindsey hid the one she was reading behind her back. "Mom?" she said, her eyes as wide as flying saucers. "Hi."

"Hello."

"Hello, Mrs. Remington," Brenda said, looking as guilty as sin itself.

It was then that Meg spied the black dress hanging from the closet door. It was probably the most provocative thing she'd seen in years.

"How'd you get the dress?" Meg demanded, angry that Lindsey had gone against her wishes and wondering how she'd managed to do it.

The two girls stared at each other and neither one seemed eager to supply the answer. "Brenda phoned her mother and she put it on her credit card," Lindsey said at last.

"What?" Meg felt ready to explode.

"It was only a small lie," Brenda said quickly, eager to smooth the waters. "I told my mom it was perfect and on sale and too good a deal to resist. What I didn't tell her was that the dress wasn't for me.''

''It's going back right this minute, and then the three of us are paying Brenda's parents a visit.''

''Mom.'' Lindsey flew off the bed. ''Wait, please.'' She had a panicked look in her eye. ''I know we did wrong, but when you didn't agree to buy the dress yourself we didn't know what to do. You just don't have anything appropriate for Chez Michelle.''

Chez Michelle was one of the most exclusive restaurants in Seattle, with a reputation for excellent French cuisine. Meg had never eaten there herself, but Lois and her husband had celebrated their silver wedding anniversary there and raved about it for weeks afterward.

''You're not making any sense,'' Meg told her daughter.

''I know.'' Lindsey bit into her lower lip.

''You have to tell her,'' Brenda insisted.

''Tell me what?''

''You were the one who wrote the last letter,'' Lindsey accused. ''The least you could have done was get the dates right.''

''It's tonight.''

''I know,'' Lindsey snapped.

''Would someone kindly tell me what's going on here?'' Meg asked with limited patience.

''You need that dress, Mom,'' Lindsey said in a voice so low Meg had to strain to hear her.

''And pray tell why?''

''You have a dinner date.''

"I do? And just who am I going out with?" She assumed this had something to do with Chez Michelle.

"Steve Conlan."

"Steve Conlan?" Meg repeated. She said it again in her mind, looking for something remotely familiar about it and finding nothing,

"You don't know him," Lindsey was quick to tell her. "But he's really nice. In fact, Brenda and I both think he's great. Really great." She looked to her friend for confirmation, and Brenda nodded eagerly.

"You've met him?" Meg didn't like the sound of this.

"Not really. We've been writing letters back and forth for almost a month and he seems like a really great guy." The last part was said with forced enthusiasm.

"You've been writing a strange man."

"He isn't so strange, Mom, not really. He sounds just like one of us."

"He wants to meet you," Brenda piped in.

"Me?" Meg flattened her hand across her breast. "Why would he want to do that?"

Once more the girls shared a look. It was reminiscent of the one she'd caught the night before, when she knew they were up to no-good.

"Lindsey?" Meg prodded. "Why would this man want to meet me?"

Her daughter lowered her gaze, refusing to meet Meg's eyes. "Because when we wrote Steve..."

"Yes," Meg urged.

"Brenda and I told him we were you."

2

$\longrightarrow\!\!\!\longleftarrow$

Steve Conlan glanced at his watch and gritted his teeth. The time hadn't changed since he'd last looked. He could tell it was going to be one of those evenings. He had the distinct feeling the entire night would drag by one interminable minute after another.

He had yet to figure how he'd gotten himself into this mess. He was minding his own business and the next thing he knew ... He didn't want to think about it, because every time he did his blood pressure rose to a dangerous level.

One thing was certain, Nancy was going to pay for this.

He was early, and not for any of the reasons a man generally arrived for a dinner date before he was due. Steve wanted this night over with as quickly as possible.

He tried not to look at the time and failed. A minute had passed. Or was it a lifetime?

The necktie felt as if it would soon strangle him, and he stuck his index finger inside the collar hoping to ease the discomfort. A tie. He couldn't believe he'd let Nancy talk him into wearing a stupid tie.

Because he needed something to do to occupy his time, he dragged the snapshot out of his shirt pocket.

Meg Remington.

She had a nice face, he decided. Nothing spectacular. She certainly wasn't drop-dead gorgeous, but she wasn't plain, either. Her eyes were her best feature, he decided. Clear. Bright. Expressive. She had a cute mouth, too. Very kissable looking. Sensuous and full.

What the hell was he supposed to say to the woman? The hell if he knew. He'd read her letters a dozen times. Maybe more. She sounded...he hated to say it, immature—as if she felt the need to impress him. She seemed to think because she ran an eight-minute mile that it qualified her for the Olympic team. Frankly, he wondered what their dinner would be like, her being so food conscious and all. She'd actually bragged about how few fat grams she consumed. Clearly she hadn't read over the menu selection at Chez Michelle. He couldn't see a single low-fat entrée.

That was another thing. The woman had expensive tastes. Dinner at Chez Michelle would set him back a hundred bucks, if he was lucky. Thus far he'd been anything but...

Involuntarily his gaze fell to his watch, and he groaned inwardly. His sister owed him for this.

Big time.

"I refuse to meet a strange man for dinner," Meg insisted, her words coated in the thickest of starch. There were some things even a mother wasn't willing to do.

"But you have to," Brenda pleaded, her pretty eyes gazing appealingly up at Meg. "I'm sorry, Mrs. Remington, I feel really bad springing you with this all at once, but Steve didn't do anything wrong. You've just got to show up. You just have to... otherwise he might lose faith in all women."

"Steve?"

"Steve Conlan, your date," Lindsey supplied. "It would have worked out great if..." she paused and glanced impatiently toward her best friend "...if one of us hadn't gotten the days mixed up."

"Just exactly when did you plan on telling me you'd been writing to a strange man, using my name?"

"Soon," Lindsey said with conviction. "We had to.... He started asking about meeting you almost right away. We did everything we could to hold him off. Oh, by the way, if he asks about your appendix, you've made a full recovery."

Meg groaned. The time frame of their deception wasn't what really interested her. She was killing time, stalling, looking for a way out of this. She could leave a message for Steve at the restaurant, explaining that she wouldn't be there, but that seemed such a cowardly thing to do.

Unfortunately no escape plan presented itself. Brenda was right—it wasn't Steve's fault that he'd been duped by a couple of teenagers. Hers, either, but then Lindsey was her daughter.

"He's really very nice looking," Brenda insisted. She reached behind her and pulled out a picture from one of the envelopes scattered across the top of Lindsey's bed. "Here, see what I mean." Meg swore she heard the teenager heave a sigh. "He's got big blue eyes and a delightful grin, kind of cocky and cute."

Meg admitted to being curious. She took the snapshot from Brenda and studied it. Her daughter's friend was right. Steve Conlan was pleasant looking enough, she supposed. His hair was a little long, but that didn't bother her. He wore a cowboy hat and boots and had his thumbs tucked into his hip pockets as he stared into the camera.

"He's tall, dark and lonesome," Lindsey supplied. Her shoulders rose with a soft, lilting sigh.

"Has he ever been married?" Meg asked, curiosity getting the better of her.

"Nope." This time it was Brenda who eagerly supplied the information. "He's got his own business, the same way as you, Mrs. Remington. He owns a body shop and he's been sinking every penny and every minute he has into it."

"What made him place the ad?" She looked to the girls and a sudden thought came to her. "He is the one who advertised, isn't he?"

Both girls looked away and Meg's heart froze. "You mean to say you two advertised for a husband for me?" Her voice wobbled like marbles scattering across a tile floor.

"We got lots of letters, too," Brenda said proudly. "We sorted through them all and chose Steve Conlan."

"Don't you want to know why?" Lindsey prodded.

Meg gestured weakly, too stunned to react one way or another.

"Steve says he decided to answer your letter because one day he woke up and realized life was passing him by. All his friends were married, and he knew something important was missing in his life. Then he knew it wasn't something but someone."

"What about female friends?" Meg asked, thinking he didn't look like a man who would stoop to find companionship in the classifieds.

"He said in a letter that..." Lindsey paused and rustled through a sheaf of papers, searching out the right envelope. "Here it is," she muttered. "He didn't have much opportunity to meet single women unless they'd been in an accident, and generally they're not in the mood for romance when they're dealing with a body shop and an insurance company." Lindsey glanced up and grinned. "He's kind of witty sometimes. I like that about him."

"He said a lot of women his age have already been married and divorced and had a passel of kids."

This didn't sound the least bit promising to Meg. "You did happen to mention that I'm a divorcée, didn't you?"

"Of course," Lindsey insisted. "We'd never lie."

Meg bit her tongue to keep from saying the obvious.

"Just think, Mrs. Remington, out of all the women he could have written, Steve chose you and we chose him. It's destiny, I tell you, pure destiny."

The girls meant for her to feel complimented, but Meg was suspicious. "Surely there was someone younger and prettier, without children, who stirred his interest."

The two girls exchanged smiles. "He liked the fact you counted fat grams," Brenda said proudly.

So much for their unwillingness to stretch the truth. "You actually told him that?" She closed her eyes and groaned. "What else did you say?"

"Just that you're really wonderful."

"Heroic, actually," Brenda added. "And you are."

Oh, great. They'd made her sound like a thin Joan of Arc.

"You will meet him, won't you?" Lindsey's round dark eyes pleaded with Meg.

"What I should do is march the two of you down to that fancy restaurant and have you personally apologize. You both deserve to be grounded until you're forty."

The girls blinked in unison, as if the thought she'd do such a thing hadn't occurred to either of them. "But, Mom..."

"Mrs. Remington..."

Meg raised her hand and stopped them from continuing. "I won't take you to Chez Michelle, and as for the grounding part...we'll discuss it later."

Two pairs of shoulders sagged with relief.

"But I won't have dinner with Steve Conlan," she said emphatically. "I'll go to the restaurant, introduce myself and explain what happened. I'm sure he'll agree that the best thing to do is to skip dinner altogether."

"You'll wear the dress, won't you?" Lindsey asked, eyeing the slinky black concoction hanging outside her closet door.

"Absolutely not," Meg said. She refused to even consider it.

"But you don't own anything special enough for Chez Michelle. Just try it on, Mom," she pleaded, as if Meg wearing that dress were all that stood between them and destitution. If she agreed, all would be well with the world; otherwise they'd both be pushing shopping carts around the streets, seeking handouts.

An hour later Meg pulled up in front of Chez Michelle wearing the very dress she'd sworn she'd never don. It fit as if it'd been specifically designed for her, emphasizing the good points in her figure and camouflaging the rest. At least that was what Lindsey and Brenda insisted.

"Hello." The hostess greeted her with a wide toothpaste-ad smile. "A table for one?"

"I'm... meeting someone," Meg told her, and glanced around the waiting area looking for a man who resembled the tall, dark and lonesome photo she carried. No one seemed to fit the description. Nor was there a single male visible wearing a cowboy hat.

The only man who vaguely resembled the photograph stood in the corner of the room, leaning indolently against the wall as if he had all the time in the world.

He straightened and stared at her.

Meg glared back at him.

He reached inside his suit pocket and took out a snapshot.

Meg opened the clasp of her purse and reached for the picture the girls had given her. She looked down at it and then up again.

He appeared to be doing the same thing.

"Meg Remington?" he asked, as if he wasn't sure even now.

"Steve Conlan?"

He nodded. "Meg Remington?"

She nodded.

He wore a suit and tie. A suit and tie. The guy had really gone all out for her. Meg swallowed uncomfortably. He'd invited her to this ultrafancy restaurant expecting to meet the woman who'd written him all those long heartfelt letters. Meg felt her heart settle somewhere in the area of her knees. She couldn't very well introduce herself and immediately say it had all been a terrible mistake and cancel dinner. Not when it was apparent he'd gone to so much trouble for this evening. It didn't seem appropriate to blurt out, five seconds after they met, that she wasn't who he thought she was.

"I believe our table is waiting," Steve said, holding out his arm to her. His hand touched her elbow and he addressed the hostess. "We're ready to be seated now."

The woman gave him an odd look, then reached for the huge tassel-laden menus. "This way."

She might have been wrong, but Meg thought she heard a bit of reluctance in his voice. Perhaps she was a disappointment to Steve Conlan. After the fitness drill Lindsey and Brenda had put her through, Meg was feeling her advancing age. She'd recently torn out a coupon from her favorite women's magazine for Oil of Olay.

Pride stiffened Meg's shoulders. So she hadn't signed any modeling contracts lately. Exactly what did he expect from a thirty-four-year-old? If he wanted to date a woman in her twenties, he shouldn't have answered her letters. Lindsey's letters, she corrected. It was all Meg could do not to stop Steve Conlan right then and there and announce this was as good as it got.

Especially in this dress. It was simply gorgeous. Meg knew now the girls had made the perfect choice. She was glad she'd given in to them on this one. Besides, Lindsey was right, she didn't own anything fancy enough for Chez Michelle. Before she could stop herself she'd agreed to wear the silly thing. Soon both girls were offering her tidbits of fashion advice.

They were escorted to a linen-covered table situated next to the window, which overlooked Elliot Bay and Puget Sound. The moon's reflection on the water sent gilded light bouncing across the surface. The restaurant's interior was dimly lit.

Meg squinted, barely able to read her menu in the poor light. She wondered if Steve was having the same problem. She hadn't originally intended to have dinner with him. Wouldn't even now, if he hadn't gone to so much trouble on her behalf. It seemed crass to drop in, announce it had all been a misguided attempt by her daughter to play matchmaker, ask his forgiveness and speedily disappear.

"I believe I'll have the chicken cordon bleu," she said, opting for the least expensive item on the menu. "And please, I insist upon paying for my own meal." It would be unforgivable to gouge him for that as well.

"Dinner is on me," Steve insisted, setting his own menu aside. He smiled for the first time and the action transformed his face. He studied her, as if he wasn't sure what to make of her. "I insist."

"But..." Meg lowered her gaze and closed her mouth. She didn't know where to start and at the same time didn't know how much longer she could maintain the pretense. "This is all very elegant...."

"Yes," he agreed, spinning the stem of his water glass between his thumb and index finger.

"You look different than your picture." Why she found it necessary to tell him that, Meg didn't know. What she should be doing was explaining about Lindsey and Brenda.

"How's that?"

"Your eyes are much bluer and you've cut your hair."

His smile was slightly off center. "Your picture didn't do you justice."

Meg hadn't thought to ask Lindsey which one she'd mailed Steve. "Can I see?"

"Sure." He pulled it out of his pocket and handed it over.

Meg took one look and rolled her eyes. She couldn't believe Lindsey would send this particular picture to anyone. It had been taken just before Christmas a year earlier. She was standing in front of the Christmas tree wearing a white dress that took all the color out of her face. The flash from the camera made her eyes appear all red. Frankly Meg thought she looked like she was recovering from a serious ailment.

"This is one of the worst pictures I've ever taken," she told him impatiently. "The one of me at the bookstore is much better."

Steve's brow creased with a frown. "I see. You should have sent that one."

Meg realized what she'd said too late. "You're right, I should have.... How silly of me."

The waitress came and they placed their order. Personally, Meg wondered how the woman could see enough to write in the dark.

Once the server had left the table, Meg smoothed the napkin across her lap. "Listen, Steve..."

"Meg..."

They both stopped.

"You go first," he insisted, gesturing toward her.

"All right." She cocked her head to one side and then the other, going over the words in her mind. "This isn't easy..."

Steve frowned. "It's been a pleasure to meet me, but the chemistry is just not right and you'd like to let me down easy now and be done with it."

"No," she hurried to assure him.

"Oh."

She hadn't a clue why he sounded so disappointed. Then she understood. "You...you're disappointed in me and..."

"Not in the least. If the truth be known, I'm pleasantly surprised."

She swallowed tightly. "I wish you hadn't said that."

"Why not?"

"Because..." She dragged in a deep breath. "Because I'm not the person you think I am. I mean..." This was proving far more difficult than it should have been. "I didn't write those letters."

Steve eyes narrowed fiercely. "Then who did?"

"My daughter and her friend."

"I see."

Meg's fingers squashed the linen napkin in her lap. "You have every reason to be upset. I wouldn't blame you in the least. It was an underhanded thing to do to us both."

"You didn't know anything about this?"

"I swear I didn't. I would have put a stop to it immediately if I had."

Steve reached for his water and drank thirstily. "I would have too, had I known."

"I want you to know I intend on disciplining Lindsey for this. I can only apologize..." She stopped midsentence when she noticed his shoulders move up and down with suppressed laughter. "Steve?"

"I didn't write those letters, either."

Disbelief settled over Meg like a heavy mantle. "You mean to say you didn't respond to the ad in Dateline?"

"Nope. My romantic little sister did. Nancy's on this kick about seeing me married. I don't understand it, personally, but..."

"Just a minute," Meg said, holding up her hand and stopping him. "Let me see if I've got this straight. You didn't place the ad in Dateline."

"You've got it."

"Then why are you here?"

He shrugged. "Probably for the same reason you are. I figured you were some lonely heart seeking companionship, and frankly I felt bad that Nancy had led you on this way. It isn't your fault my nutcake of a sister thinks it's long past time I got married."

He paused when their meals were delivered.

Meg dug into her chicken with gusto. Irritation usually made her overly hungry. She stabbed the half-cooked carrot slices with her fork.

"So you felt sorry for me?" she said, chewing the carrot as if it were raw and in need of crunching.

He looked up, apparently sensing her irritation. "No more sorry that you felt for me."

He had her there.

"It's the reason you showed up, isn't it?" he pressed.

She agreed with a nod. "When did you find out about this dinner date?"

"This morning. You?"

She looked at her watch. "About two hours ago."

Steve chuckled. "They didn't give you much opportunity to object, did they?"

"Actually they got the days mixed up and went into a small panic. I don't suppose you happened to read any of the letters they wrote?"

"As a matter of fact I did. Interesting stuff."

"I'll bet." She stabbed at one of the potato pieces and captured it on the end of her fork. "You should know not everything they said was the truth." She stuffed the potato in her mouth and chewed as if it were leather.

"So you don't actually run an eight-minute mile."

"Not exactly."

"Nine minutes?"

"I don't exactly run, and before you ask me about fat grams you can forget everything Lindsey told you about those, too. And for the record, my appendix is in great shape."

Steve chuckled. "What did Nancy tell you about me?"

"Being that I've only read tidbits of your letters this evening, I can't rightly say."

"Oh?" He sounded downright disappointed.

"As I recall, your sister did say something along the lines of your life being empty and you looking for something to fill your lonely nights..." she paused for effect "...then you realized it wasn't something you were searching to find but someone."

His jaw tightened. "She said that?"

"Yup." Meg took a good deal of delight in telling him that.

"Well that's a crock of bull, if I ever heard it. I certainly hope you didn't believe it."

Meg was almost beginning to enjoy this. "Not really. Lindsey didn't mean any harm."

"Nancy, either, although I'd like to personally throttle her. The kid's just turned nineteen and she's got romance on the mind. Unfortunately, it's me she plans to marry off."

"Lindsey thinks I'm lost and lonely, but I'm perfectly content with my life."

"Me, too."

"Why ruin everything now?"

"Exactly," Steve agreed with conviction. "A woman would only mess with my mind."

"A man would string me along until he found someone prettier and sexier. Besides," Meg added, "I have no intention of becoming a pawn to my daughter's whims."

"Nancy can take a flying leap into Green Lake before I'll let her arrange my love life," Steve told her adamantly. "I fully intend to marry, but on my time—not when my kid sister ropes me into a lonely-hearts-club relationship."

"I feel the same way."

"Great." Steve grinned at her, and Meg had to admit he had a perfectly wonderful smile. It lit up his eyes, softened his features and added to the rough-hewn appeal. "Shall we drink to our agreement?"

"That sounds like a great idea."

Steve attracted the waitress's attention and ordered a bottle of wine.

It surprised Meg how easily they could talk, once all the pretense between them had been resolved. She found herself telling him about her bookstore and enjoyed hearing about his body shop. They lingered over coffee and dessert, and it wasn't until it became apparent that the restaurant was about to close that they stood to leave.

"I enjoyed myself," Meg told him as they strolled toward the door.

"Don't sound so surprised."

"Frankly, I am."

He chuckled. "I guess I am, too."

The valet delivered her Ford Escort to the front of the restaurant and held open her car door. Their evening was drawing to a close.

"Thank you for a wonderful dinner," she said, suddenly feeling shy and awkward.

"The pleasure was all mine."

Neither of them made the effort to move. The valet looked at his watch and Meg glanced guiltily toward him. Steve ignored him and eventually so did Meg.

"I guess this is goodbye," she said, wishing now that she hadn't made such a big issue about not being her daughter's pawn.

"It looks that way."

She lowered her gaze, fighting the lure she read in his. "Thanks again."

Steve traced his finger along the underside of her jaw. His work-calloused fingertip felt like warm silk against her tender skin. If they hadn't been standing under the lights in front of a fancy French restaurant with a valet looking on, Meg wondered if he might have kissed her. She would like to think he might have.

On the drive home, she dismissed the idea as fanciful. It had been a good, long while since she'd been wined and dined. Or kissed.

Sensation after warm sensation traveled across her face where he'd touched her. Smile after smile flirted with her mouth at the memory of his lips so close to her own. She wouldn't forget the date or the man any time soon. That was for sure.

"Well, how'd it go?" Nancy demanded. His teen-age sister met Steve at his front door. Her eyes were wide and expectant as she followed him inside the house like a puppy dog, eager for details.

Steve looked at his watch and frowned. "What are you still doing up?"

Nancy's face fell. "As I recall you asked me to wait for you, so we could talk."

Steve slid his fingers though his hair. "I did, didn't I?"

"You're much later than you thought you'd be."

He didn't respond, unwilling for his sister to know how much he'd enjoyed himself. "I should have you skinned alive for what you did," he said, forcing his voice to sound gruff with irritation.

"Maybe," she agreed readily enough.

"Haven't you got schoolwork you should be doing?" He barked, jerking the tie back and forth several times in an effort to loosen it.

"You liked her, didn't you?"

Nancy sounded too damn smug to suit Steve.

"And no I don't have any schoolwork, and you know it. School let out two weeks ago."

"So you've decided to stay in Seattle and make my life miserable."

"No, I've decided to stay in Seattle and see you married. Come on, Steve, you're thirty-five. That's getting up there, you know." She flopped back down on the sofa and sat with her legs under her, as if she planned to plant herself right there until he announced his engagement.

The problem, Steve decided, was that Nancy was the product of parents who had never expected a second child and had spoiled her senseless. He was partially to blame, as well, but he'd never expected she'd pull something like this.

"You work too hard," she insisted. "It's time to loosen up and enjoy life a little."

"You're going to write Mrs. Remington a letter of apology." He refused to give ground on this.

"All right, all right. I'll write her." All at once she was on her feet. "When are you seeing her again?"

"I'm not."

Nancy fell back onto the sofa cushion. "Why aren't you?"

The hell if Steve could give her an answer. Meg and he'd decided that early on in their conversation, and for the life of him he couldn't remember why.

"Because," he growled. "Now leave me alone."

Nancy threw back her head and laughed gleefully. "You like her. You really, really like her."

Meg sat in the back storeroom and rubbed her aching feet. The shoes pinched her toes, but this was what she got for being a slave to fashion. Lindsey had suggested the shoes that morning, and even knowing her feet would pay the penalty later Meg had opted to wear them.

Lois stuck her head through the door and smiled when she saw her. "A beautiful bouquet of flowers just arrived for you," she said.

"For me?"

"That's what the envelope said."

"From who?"

"I didn't read the card, if that's what you're asking, but Lindsey's here and she grabbed it first thing and let out a holler. My guess is the flowers are from Steve.''

''Steve.'' Pain or no pain, Meg was on her feet. She hobbled to the front of the store and found her fifteen-year-old daughter grinning triumphantly ear to ear.

''Steve Conlan sent flowers,'' she crowed.

''So I see.'' Meg's fingers shook as she removed the card from the small envelope.

''He said, and I quote. 'You're one special woman, Meg Remington. Love, Steve.' ''

The bouquet was huge, with at least ten different varieties of flowers all arranged in a white wicker basket. It must have cost him a hundred dollars.

''We agreed,'' she whispered, not knowing what to think.

''To what?'' Lindsey prodded.

''That we weren't going to see each other again.''

''Apparently he changed his mind,'' Lindsey said, as if she'd just discovered a sock full of money in the bottom of her purse.

Unwilling to trust her daughter's assessment of the situation, Meg stared at her best friend.

''Don't look at me,'' Lois said.

''I'm sure you're wrong,'' Meg said to Lindsey. It took a moment for her heart to stop pounding. One would think Lindsey and Brenda had managed to drag her back onto the high-school track, the way her heart had reacted to a silly bouquet of flowers.

''Why else would he send flowers?'' Lindsey asked in a calm, reasonable tone of voice.

"He wanted to tell me he was pleased we'd met, that's all. I don't think we should make something out of it that it isn't," she said, as if she were a proven mindreader.

"Call him," Lindsey pleaded.

"I most certainly will not."

"But Mom, don't you see? Steve's saying he likes you, but that he doesn't want to pressure you into anything unless you like him, too."

"He is?" Whatever confidence she'd felt moments earlier vanished like ice cream at a Fourth of July picnic.

"The next move is yours."

"Lois?"

"I wouldn't know," her fickle friend said. "I've been married to the same man for twenty-six years. All this intrigue is beyond me."

"I agree with your daughter." A shy voice said from the other side of the counter. "You should phone him."

It was Meg's customer, Mrs. Wilson. Meg wasn't sure she should listen to the older woman who faithfully purchased romance novels twice a month. Mrs. Wilson had a romantic heart and was sure to read more into the gesture than Steve ever intended.

"See," Lindsey said excitedly. "The ball's in your court. Steve made his move and is waiting for yours."

Meg didn't know what to think.

"It's been three days," Lindsey reminded her in a soft singsong voice. "He's had time to think over the situation and so have you."

"Call him," Lois advised. "If for nothing more than to thank him for the flowers."

"It's the least you can do." Once more it was her daughter offering her advice.

"All right," Meg agreed reluctantly. The flowers were lovely, and thanking him would be the proper thing to do.

"I'll get his work number for you," Lindsey volunteered, pulling the Yellow Pages from the slot behind the cash register.

The kid had Steve's shop number faster than directory assistance could have located it.

"I'll use the phone in the back room," Meg announced. The last thing she wanted was to have several sets of ears listening in on her conversation.

She felt everyone's eyes follow her as she made her way into the storeroom. Her hand actually shook as she punched out the telephone number.

"Emerald City," a gruff male voice answered.

"Hello, this is Meg Remington calling for Steve Conlan."

"Hold on a minute?"

"Of course," she answered politely.

A moment later, Steve was on the line. "Meg?"

"Hello, Steve. I know you're busy, so I won't take up much of your time. I'm calling to thank you for the lovely bouquet of flowers."

A long pause followed her words. "Flowers? What flowers?"

3

——▶◀——

"**Y**ou mean to say you don't know anything about these flowers?" Meg cried, her voice raised and sounding, even to her own ears, slightly irrational. Steve could see that he hadn't done a very good job of breaking the news, but frankly he was as shocked as she was.

"If you didn't send them, who did?" Meg demanded, as if she'd been deeply wronged.

Steve didn't need to be a rocket scientist to figure that one out. "I can make a wild guess," he said with heavy sarcasm. He jerked his fingers through his hair, then glanced at the wall clock. It was close to quitting time. "Can you meet me?"

"Why?"

Her blatant lack of enthusiasm irritated him no end. For three days he'd done damn little but think about her. Nancy was right—he had liked Meg Remington. She was a bit eccentric and a little on the hysterical side, but he was willing to look past that. In mentally reviewing their time together, he was struck by her intelligence and her warmth. More than once he'd wished they'd decided to look past the way they'd been thrown together and continue seeing each other. Apparently Meg suffered no such regrets and was pleased to be rid of him.

"Why do you want to meet?" she repeated, lowering her voice to a husky whisper.

"We need to talk."

"Where?"

"How about a drink? Can you get away from the store in the next hour or so?"

She hesitated. "I'll try."

Steve mentioned a popular sports bar in Kent, and she agreed to meet him there at five-thirty. His spirits lifted considerably knowing he'd be seeing her again. He must have been smiling because his foreman, Gary Wilcox, cast him a puzzled look.

"I didn't know you had yourself a new lady friend," Gary said, when Steve turned away from the phone. "When did all this happen?"

"It hasn't." The last thing Steve needed was Gary feeding false information to his sister. Nancy and her wacky ideas about marrying him off was enough of a problem, without Gary adding to it.

"It hasn't happened yet, you mean," Gary said, making a notation in the appointment schedule.

Steve glanced over the other man's shoulder, to be sure Gary wasn't making notes about the conversation he'd had with Meg. Good grief, he was getting paranoid already. A woman did that to a man, he knew that much from past experience. They were known to seriously mess up a man's mind, not to mention the havoc they played on one's generally pleasant disposition.

An hour later Steve sat in front of a big-screen television with a frosty mug of beer in his hand. The booth was in the far corner of the room, where he could easily see the front door.

Meg walked in no more than ten minutes after him. At least Steve thought she appeared to be Meg. The woman carried a tennis racket and wore one of those cute pleated-skirt outfits as if she had recently stepped off the court.

Steve squinted and stared, unsure. After all, he'd only seen her the one time, and in the slinky black dress she'd looked a whole lot different.

Meg solved his problem for him when she apparently recognized him. She walked across the room, and he noticed she limped. Sliding into the booth next to him, she set the tennis racket on top of the table.

"Lindsey knows," she announced, and her shoulders sagged forward.

Steve's head went back to study her. "I beg your pardon?"

"My daughter figured it out."

Steve hated to be so dense, but he hadn't a clue what she was talking about. "Figured out what?"

"That I was meeting you," she said, as if it should have been more than obvious. "First off, I telephoned you from the back room at the store, so our conversation could be private."

"So?"

She glared at him. "Then I made up this ridiculous story about a tennis match I'd forgotten. I haven't played tennis in years and Lindsey knows that. Immediately she had all these questions. She saw straight through me.'' She jerked the sweatband from her hair and stuffed it inside her purse. ''She's probably home right now laughing her head off at me. I can't do this.... I never was able to lie convincingly.''

Steve hadn't meant for her to go through so much trouble. ''Why didn't you just tell your daughter the truth?''

The look of consternation Meg tossed him said that would have been impossible. ''Well... because Lindsey would place some significance in the two of us meeting.''

''Why would she do that? You told her I wasn't the one who wrote the letters, didn't you?''

''No.''

''Why not?''

Meg's index finger played with the worn strings of the tennis racket as her gaze avoided his. ''I should have.... I mean, the whole thing is kind of crazy.''

''You can say that again.'' He tried to sound flippant and nonchalant, and wondered if he'd pulled it off. He didn't think he had. If the truth be known, he'd been rather amused by the whole setup. Her daughter and his sister. It was no wonder those two had gotten along like gangbusters. They were close in age and obviously spoke the same language.

''Lindsey's still got visions of sugarplums dancing in her head when it comes to men and romance and...'' Meg paused and chanced a look at him. ''...I kind of hated to be the one to disillusion her. Although heaven knows after what she did, she deserves what she gets.''

''What did you say about our date?''

Meg's hands returned to the tennis racket. "I didn't tell her much."

Steve hadn't been willing to discuss many of the details of their evening together with Nancy, either. Nothing had surprised him more than discovering how attractive he'd found Meg Remington. It wasn't solely a sexual attraction, either, although she certainly physically appealed to him.

In the past three days, when he thought about her, it wasn't her womanly attributes that rushed to his memory. She'd pop into his mind and he'd remember the way they'd talked nonstop over the wine and dessert. He remembered how she'd gotten wrapped up in what he was saying and had leaned forward and then realized her dress revealed an abundant display of cleavage. Red-faced, she'd pulled back and attempted to adjust her top.

Steve liked the way her eyes brightened when she spoke of her bookstore and her daughter, and the quirky way she had of holding her breath when she was excited about something, as if she'd forgotten to breathe.

"Your sister . . . the one who wrote the letters is the same one who sent the flowers?" Meg asked, breaking into his thoughts.

Steve nodded. "That's my guess."

Meg fiddled with the clasp of her purse and brought out a small card which she handed to him.

Steve raised his arm to attract the cocktail waitress's attention and indicate he wanted another beer for Meg.

''I shouldn't,'' she said and reached for a pretzel. ''If I come home with beer on my breath Lindsey will know for sure I wasn't playing tennis.''

''According to you, she's already figured it out.''

She slid the bowl of pretzels her way and reached for a handful. ''That's true.''

Steve opened the card that had come with the flowers and rolled his eyes. ''This is from Nancy, all right,'' he muttered. ''I'd never write anything this hokey.''

The waitress came with another frosty mug of beer and Steve paid for it. ''Do you want more pretzels?'' he asked Meg.

''Please.'' Then in a lower voice, she added, ''This type of situation always makes me hungry.''

She licked the salt from her fingertips. ''Have…has my daughter, Lindsey, been in contact with you?''

''No, but then I'm not likely to know that, am I?''

The pretzel was poised in front of Meg's mouth. ''Why wouldn't you?''

''Because Lindsey would be writing to Nancy.''

Meg's head dropped in a gesture of defeat. ''You're right. Much more of this craziness and heaven only knows what they could do with our lives.''

''We need to take control,'' Steve said.

''I couldn't agree with you more,'' was her response. She took a sip of the beer and set the mug back down on the table. ''I shouldn't be drinking this on an empty stomach—it'll go straight to my head.''

''The bar's got great sandwiches.''

''Pretzels are fine.'' Apparently she had realized all at once that she was holding the bowl, and she shoved it back to the center of the table. "Sorry," she muttered.

"No problem."

He saw her wince and remembered she'd been limping earlier. "Is there something wrong with your foot?"

"The shoes I wore to work were too tight," she said in a voice so low he had to strain to hear.

"Here," he said, reaching for her legs and setting them on his lap.

"What are you doing?" she asked, as if she expected him to pull out a switchblade.

"I thought I'd rub them for you."

"You'd do that?"

"Yes." It didn't seem so odd a thing to him. The fact was, he hated to see her in pain. "Besides, we need to talk over how we're going to handle this situation. I have the feeling that we're going to have to be in top mental form to deal with these kids."

"You're right." She closed her eyes and purred like a well-fed kitten when he removed her shoes and kneaded the bottoms of her aching feet.

"Feel better?" he asked after a couple of moments.

She nodded and her eyes remained closed. "I think you should stop," she said, sounding completely unconvincing.

"Why?" He asked the question, but he stopped and handed her back her shoes. Actually, Steve didn't know what had possessed him. He'd never done anything like this before. Generally, if a woman's feet hurt it was her problem, not his. But he knew that Meg often had to stand for hours on end. His feet hurt just thinking about it.

"Thank you," Meg said, and looked around a little self-consciously as she slipped her shoes back on and quickly tied the laces.

Feeling thoroughly embarrassed by his uncharacteristic response to her, Steve cleared his throat and reached for his beer. "Do you have any ideas?" he asked.

She looked at him as if she hadn't a clue what he was talking about, then abruptly straightened. "Oh, you mean in dealing with the kids. No, not really. What about you? Any suggestions?"

"First off, we've got to stop letting them run our lives."

"I couldn't agree with you more."

Steve nodded once. "We aren't puppets."

"Exactly."

If that were the case, he wondered, why did he experience the uncanny desire to kiss her? It distressed him that they could carry on a conversation that would ensure they'd not be troubled with each other again. At the same instant, he couldn't help wondering about the taste of her mouth. Steve speculated that it would be sweet. Cotton-candy sweet. Salty too, from the pretzels. The combination had always been his favorite.

There's something wrong with this picture, Conlan, he said to himself, but he couldn't keep from studying her.

He'd been wrong about her face, he decided. She was lovely, with classic features. He'd trailed his finger down the curve of her cheek the first time they'd met, and now he did so a second time, mentally.

She knew what he was thinking. Steve swore she did. Her pulse hammered wildly in the vein in her throat and she looked away.

Steve did, as well. He didn't know what was happening, didn't want to know. He reached for his beer and gulped down two deep swallows. What he really needed was a medical professional. Preferably one in the mental-health field. Rubbing her feet, thinking about kissing her. The last thing he wanted messing up his life was a woman.

Especially one such as Meg Remington.

"So you met Steve again," Lois said calmly. They sat on a bench in Lincoln Park enjoying huge rocky road ice-cream cones. A ferry eased toward the dock at Fauntleroy.

"Who told you that?" Meg answered, deciding to play dumb.

"Lindsey, who else? You really didn't think you'd fooled her, did you?"

"No." Clearly she had no talent for subterfuge.

"Tell me how your meeting went."

Meg didn't answer for a long time. She couldn't. There weren't words to tell her friend about her meeting with Steve. Even now she wasn't sure what good, if any, they'd accomplished. What disturbed her was her willingness, her eagerness to see Steve again.

In retrospect she saw that it was a mistake for them to get together. All she could think about was how he'd lifted her legs onto his lap and rubbed the tired achiness away. They'd been talking, and then for no reason she could explain there was this sudden explosion of awareness between them. This living, breathing, throbbing awareness.

Rarely had Meg wanted a man to kiss her more. For the love of heaven, right in the middle of a sports bar. It was the craziest, most uncanny thing to happen to her in years. That of itself was distressing, but what happened afterward baffled her even more.

Melting ice cream dripped onto her hand and Meg hurriedly licked it away.

"Meg?" Lois said, studying her. "Something's wrong, isn't there?"

"No," she said, laughing off her friend's concern. "What could possibly be wrong?"

"You haven't been yourself the last couple of days."

"Sure I have," she countered, then knowing it would do no good to continue to pretend, she blurted out the truth. "I'm afraid I could really fall for this guy."

Lois laughed. "What's so awful about that?"

"For one thing, he isn't interested in me."

This time Lois eyed her suspiciously. "What makes you think that?"

"Several reasons."

Lois took the first bite out of the side of her waffle cone. "Name one."

"First off he wanted to meet so we could come up with a way to keep the kids from manipulating our lives."

"That sounds suspiciously like an excuse to see you again," Lois told her.

"Trust me, it wasn't. Steve did everything but come right out and say that he isn't keen on dating me."

"You're sure about this?"

"Of course, I am. There was ample opportunity for him to suggest we get to know each other better, and he didn't." She'd assumed Steve had experienced the same physical attraction she had, but apparently she'd been wrong.

Lindsey and Brenda had insisted she still had it. Meg hated to argue with them, but recent experience had proven otherwise. Whatever it was had long since deserted her.

"Did it occur to you that he might have been waiting for you to suggest something?" Lois asked.

"No," Meg responded frankly. Steve wasn't a man who took his cues from a woman. If he wanted something or someone, he'd make it known. If he were looking for a way to continue to see her, he would have told her.

"There's got to be more than that."

"There is," Meg assured her. "I was just getting ready to tell you. Steve came up with the idea originally, but I was the one who agreed."

"Agreed? To what?"

Meg stood and found the closest garbage receptacle to dump what remained of her ice cream. "Before I tell you, remember that I'd been drinking beer on an empty stomach."

"This doesn't sound promising," Lois said to no one in particular.

"It isn't." Drawing in a deep breath, she sat back down on the park bench next to her friend. "The more we talked the more it became apparent that the louder we protested we weren't attracted to each other, the less likely either Lindsey or Nancy will believe us.''

''There's a problem with this scenario.''

''There is?'' Meg questioned.

''Yes, and we both know what it is. You're interested in Steve. Very interested.'' Lois gave her a look that said Meg hadn't fooled her.

Meg looked away. ''I don't want to confuse the issue with that.''

''All right, go on,'' Lois said, although she already looked thoroughly baffled.

''Steve thought the only possible way we had of convincing Lindsey that he wasn't the right person for me was if he started dating me and...''

''See,'' Lois said triumphantly. ''He is interested. Real interested. Don't you get it? This idea of his is an excuse.''

''I doubt it.'' Meg could see no reason for him to play games if that were the case. ''You can come over this evening if you want, and see for yourself.''

''See what for myself?''

''Steve's coming to meet Lindsey.''

''To your house?''

''Yes.''

Lois's grin resembled that of a cheshire cat. ''R-e-a-l-l-y,'' she said, dragging out the word.

''Really. But trust me, it isn't what you think.'' Her friend was in for a major disappointment.

Meg was home an hour later. It was clear Lindsey had taken Steve's visit seriously. The teenager had cleaned the house, baked cookies and was dressed in her best jeans. A dress would have been asking for too much.

"Hello, sweetheart."

"Mom," Lindsey said, looking at her watch. "Do you have any idea what time it is?"

"Yeah."

"Don't you think you should shower and change clothes? Steve will be here in an hour and a half."

"I know." She supposed she should reveal more enthusiasm for this, if only for show, but she couldn't make herself do it. This had been Steve's idea and she'd agreed, but frankly none of this sat well with her.

"I was thinking you should wear that sundress we bought last year with the pretty red-rose print," Lindsey suggested. "That and your white sandals." She tapped her finger against her chin. "I wish you owned one of those broad-brimmed hats. A pretty white one would be perfect."

"We'll just have to make do with the sombrero Grandpa bought you in Mexico," Meg teased.

"Mother," Lindsey cried, appalled. "That would look ridiculous."

Meg sighed dramatically, for effect. "I don't know how I managed to dress all these years without you."

She thought—or hoped—that Lindsey would laugh. Her daughter didn't. "It might well be the reason you're still single. Have you thought of that?"

This kid wasn't worth beans when it came to boosting her confidence.

"You're a great mother," Lindsey said, redeeming herself somewhat, "but promise me you'll never go clothes shopping without me again."

Rather than make rash pledges she had no intention of keeping, Meg hurried up the stairs and stepped into the shower. The hot water pulsating against her skin refreshed her and renewed her sense of humor. She could hardly wait to see Lindsey's face when she met Steve.

With a towel tucked around her, Meg wandered into her bedroom and reviewed the contents of her closet. The sundress was her best choice. She wore it, Meg told herself, because it looked good on her and not because Lindsey had suggested it.

Her daughter was waiting for her in the living room. The floral arrangement Steve, or rather Nancy, had sent was displayed in the middle of the coffee table.

Lindsey had buffed and polished the sterling silver set until it gleamed. The previous time Meg had used it had been when Pastor Delany had come for a visit shortly after Meg's father had died.

When the doorbell chimed, Lindsey looked to her mother and grinned broadly. "We're ready," she said, and gave her a thumbs-up sign.

Meg had thought she knew what to expect, but when she opened the front door her mouth sagged open.

"Steve?" she whispered to the man dressed in a black leather jacket and skin-tight blue jeans. His white T-shirt was thin and revealed a smattering of dark chest hairs. "Is that you?"

He winked at her. "You expecting someone else?"

"No-o-o," she stammered.

"Invite me in," he suggested and when she stepped aside, he walked past her and stuck his index finger under her chin, closing her mouth.

He stood in the archway between the entryway and her living room and braced his feet apart. "You must be Lindsey," he said in a gruff voice. "I'm Steve."

"You're Steve?" Lindsey repeated in a meek voice and stared at Meg.

"Lindsey this is Steve Conlan," Meg said, and stood next to the man her daughter had arranged for her to meet.

Steve wrapped his arm around Meg's trim waist and planted a noisy kiss on her cheek. He glanced at Lindsey. "I understand you're the one responsible for getting the two of us together? Those were some letters you wrote."

"Thank you." Lindsey's eyes didn't so much as flicker. She certainly wasn't about to let them read her thoughts. "You don't look anything like your picture."

Steve refused to take his eyes off Meg. He squeezed her waist again. "The one I sent was taken a while back," he said. "Before I was in prison."

Lindsey gasped. "Prison?"

"Don't worry, sweetheart. There isn't a violent bone in my body."

"What...were you in for?" Lindsey asked, her voice shaking.

Steve rubbed the side of his jaw and bounced his gaze off Meg's daughter. "If you don't mind, I'd rather not say."

"Sit down, Steve," Meg said between gritted teeth. Talk about overkill. Much more of this and everything would be ruined.

"Would you care for coffee?" Lindsey asked, and her young voice continued to tremble.

"You got a beer?"

"It's not a good idea for you to be drinking this early in the afternoon is it?" Meg asked sweetly.

Steve sat down on the sofa and lifted his leg, balancing his ankle over his knee. He looked around as if he were casing the joint.

Meg moved to the silver service. "Coffee or tea?"

"Coffee, but add a little something to it that'll give it some kick."

Meg poured coffee for him and added a generous measure of half-and-half. He looked at the delicate bone china cup as if he wasn't sure how to hold it.

Lindsey sat down on the ottoman, her eyes growing larger by the minute. "I . . . you never said anything about prison."

"Don't like to mention it until a person's had a chance to meet me for themselves. A lot of people tend to think the worst about a person when they hear about a felony conviction."

"A felony conviction." Lindsey snapped her mouth closed, inhaled sharply, then said in a subdued tone, "I see."

"The flowers are lovely," Meg said, fingering a rosebud from the delicate bouquet.

Steve grinned. "My probation officer told me women like that sort of thing. Glad to know he was right." He sipped from the coffee and made a small slurping sound. "By the way, you'll be glad to hear I told him about you and me, and he did a background check on you and said it was fine for the two of us to continue to date each other."

"That's wonderful," Meg said.

Steve set aside the delicate cup and leaned forward, bracing his elbows against his knees. He stared at Lindsey and smiled. "I got to thank you," he said, his eyes dark and serious. "I realize your mother's upset with you placing that ad and you writing me all those letters. Generally, it's not a good idea to fool someone that way, but I wasn't being completely honest with you either, so I guess we're even."

Lindsey nodded.

"Your mother's one special woman, just the way I said in the card I sent with the flowers. There aren't a lot of females who'd be willing to look past my lawless nature. Most women don't know or care that I've got a heart as pure as gold. Your mama did. We sat down in that fancy restaurant and I took one look at her pretty face and I knew she was the woman for me." He rubbed the side of his unshaved jaw and laughed. "I do have to tell you, though, that when you suggested Chez Michelle I was afraid that Meg just might be too high maintenance for someone like me."

"I'm sorry..." Lindsey floundered with the apology. "I didn't know."

"Don't you fret. Your mama was worth every penny of that fancy dinner. Just getting to know her and love her, why a man couldn't ask for a prettier filly." He eyed her as if she were a Thanksgiving feast, then moistened his lips as if it were all he could do to keep from grabbing her right then and there and kissing her long and hard.

"Steve . . ." Meg muttered.

"I know, I know," he said, and seemed to pull himself together. "Earl Markum, my probation officer, says I've got to be careful not to rush matters between us. I apologize. I look at your beautiful eyes and I can't seem to help myself."

"Yes, well . . ."

"You didn't tell me how good-looking your daughter is," he said, as if Meg had purposely been holding out on him.

"Lindsey's my pride and joy," Meg said, beaming her daughter a smile.

"I got plenty of friends who wouldn't mind meeting a good-looking young lady like you." He winked at Lindsey as if to say all he needed was one word from her and he'd make the arrangements himself.

"Absolutely not," Meg said forcefully, forgetting this was all a game. "I won't have you introducing my daughter to your friends."

Steve's eyes widened with surprise and he held up his right hand, as if swearing to something sacred. "Sorry, I didn't mean to offend. You don't want Lindsey dating any of my buddies, then fine, I'll see that it never happens."

"Good." Meg had to hand it to Steve, he was an excellent actor. He almost had her believing him. She suspected that was because he'd turned himself into the man she'd half expected to meet that night.

Steve smacked his lips. "I got to tell you when I first saw Margaret in that pretty black dress, my heart went all the way to the floor. She was the most beautiful woman I've seen since I was released.'' His eyes softened as his gaze fell on Meg.

"Released?" Lindsey squeaked.

"From prison," Steve clarified, his gaze immediately returning to Meg.

It would help matters considerably if he didn't look so damn sincere.

"Yes, well..." Meg said, standing. Once she was on her feet she didn't know what she was going to do.

"I suspect you want me to take you on that motorcycle ride I been promising you," Steve said, downing the last of his coffee. He kept his little finger elevated as if he were sipping tea with the queen of England herself.

"Mom's going on a motorcycle with you?" Lindsey asked. Her throat muscles moved up and down.

"I'd better change clothes," Meg said, eager to escape so she could speak to Steve alone.

"No need," Steve said. "You can ride sidesaddle if you want. I brought my Hog. There's plenty of room, although I got to tell you, I been dreaming about you cuddling up and wrapping your arms around my middle. You'll need to hold on tight, honey, real tight." His eyes didn't waver from hers, and the sexual innuendo was heavy.

"Yes, well..." Either the room had grown considerably warmer or Meg was in deep trouble.

From the look of disgust Lindsey cast her, she could see it was the latter.

"I think I'll change into a pair of jeans, if it's all the same to you."

"No problem," Steve said and wiped the back of his hand across his mouth. "Just don't keep me waiting long, you hear?"

"I won't," she promised.

Meg rushed toward the stairs, anxious to get away.

Steve reached out and stopped her. His hand closed over her shoulder and he brought her into his arms. She released a gasp of surprise. Without giving her time to recover, he lowered his mouth to hers.

It was all for show, but that didn't keep her heart from fluttering wildly. Her stomach muscles tightened at the unexpectedness of his kiss.

Her lips parted and she slid her arms tightly around his hard, narrow waist. Steve groaned and forced her mouth open wider.

Meg feared the hunger she felt in him was a reflection of her own. By the time he dragged his lips from hers they were both panting. Speechless, they stared at each other.

"I'll . . . I'll be right back," she managed in a broken whisper and raced up the stairs as if the demons of hell were in hot pursuit.

4

The minute they were alone outside, Meg hit Steve across his upper arm. Her hand connected with his powerful muscles and stung unmercifully. Biting into her lower lip, she jerked her fingers back and forth several times, then gripped her hand protectively and held it against her breasts.

"What was that for?" Steve demanded, glaring at her.

"You overdid it," she flared, barely understanding her own outrage.

"I had to convince her I was unsuitable, didn't I?"

Meg bristled and attempted to rub the numbness from her fingers. "Yes, but you went above and beyond what we discussed. All that business about me being so beautiful and how I took your breath away," she muttered as she walked to the driveway where he'd parked the Harley-Davidson. She climbed onto the leather seat without thinking.

"I thought I did a wonderful job," Steve argued. A smile flirted at the edges of his sensuous mouth.

"That's another thing," she said, unable to stop looking at him. "Was that kiss really necessary?"

"Yes," he said calmly, but Meg could tell that he didn't take kindly to her rebuke. "Lindsey needed to see me in action," he insisted.

"You frightened my daughter half out of her wits as it was. There was no need to..."

Steve eyes widened, then softened into a smile. "You liked the kiss," he said flatly. "You liked it and now you aren't sure what to do."

"Don't be ridiculous. You had your tongue halfway down my throat. It...it was disgusting."

"No it wasn't." His smile was cocky and full. He laughed then, the timbre low and mildly threatening. "Maybe I should prove to you how wrong you are."

Meg shifted uncomfortably in the rear of the seat. "Let's get this over with," she said, feigning boredom. "You're going to take me out for an hour or so and then drive me back. Right? By the way, where did you get the motorcycle?"

He advanced a step toward her. "It's mine."

"Yours?" He was exactly the type of man her mother had warned her about and here she was flirting with danger. He moved a step closer and she swallowed tightly.

"You don't know much about men, do you?" he asked, his voice low and husky.

"I was married for nearly six years," she primly informed him. He was close now, too close for comfort. She kept her spine stiff and her eyes directed straight ahead. If the motorcycle was his, it was reasonable to assume that the leather jacket belonged to him as well. The persona that he'd taken on, the criminal element, might not be too far from the truth.

"You haven't been with a man since, have you?"

She felt the breathy words against her flushed face. "I refuse to answer questions of a personal nature," she returned, her words as tight as new shoes.

"You haven't," he returned confidently. "Look at me, Meg."

"No. Let's get this ride over with."

"Look at me," he insisted.

She tried to resist, but the words were warm and hypnotic. Against her better judgment, she twisted toward him. "Yes?" she asked, her heart pounding so loud and hard it felt as if it were about to hammer straight through her chest.

He wove his hands into her hair and tilted her head so that she couldn't avoid staring up at him. His gaze bored relentlessly into hers.

"Admit it," he whispered. "You enjoyed the kiss." His eyes were magnificent, she admitted reluctantly, resisting him every step.

"How like a man to link a silly kiss with his ego," she said in an effort to make light of what had transpired between them.

Steve frowned.

Meg battled a fluttery feeling in the pit of her stomach, the same kind of feeling that had attacked her when he'd kissed her by the staircase. She felt vulnerable and helpless.

"For your information, I didn't have my tongue halfway down your throat," he said, in what she was sure was a deceptively normal voice. "But it was what we both wanted."

"You're nuts," she whispered, hurrying to assure him that he'd been wrong. Very wrong. She lowered her gaze, but this proved to be a tactical error. Before she realized what he intended, he was kissing her again. His mouth possessively captured her.

Meg wanted to protest. If she'd fought him, struggled, he might have released her. She'd like to think he would have, but she couldn't be sure. Her one weak objection came in the form of a moan. This however appeared to encourage him rather than dissuade him.

His tongue flirted with her lips, and when she relaxed ever so slightly he took full advantage and brazenly entered her mouth. Without invitation he quickly involved her in blatantly provocative things, erotic games; his tongue curling around hers, dancing with hers, teasing, tasting, tantalizing.

All at once it was important that they be closer. Meg wasn't sure how it happened, but before long she was kneeling on the leather cushion and Steve's arms were wrapped around her middle. They didn't stay there long. He glided his hands down the length of her back and onto the swell of her buttocks, urging her to fit her softness against him.

Meg didn't require much inducement. Her body willfully molded itself against him. Her pliant flesh slid against the solid muscles of his chest and thighs. Only his chest and thighs weren't the only things as hard as rock.

Her eyes fluttered open and with a determined effort she broke free. Steve resisted, his arms tightening like a vise before he relaxed and released her.

"Dear God," he whispered, but Meg had the clear impression this wasn't a salutation to a prayer.

For her own part, Meg was having a difficult time breathing. Sensations swarmed through her, bothersome ones. Steve made her feel as if she'd never been kissed before now, never been held or loved. Never been married or shared intimacies with a man.

She blinked a couple of times, and Steve backed away as if he didn't know what to say. His face was tight with a frown and he jerked his fingers through his hair, holding his hands there while he seemed to sort through his own troubled emotions.

"I suppose you're looking for me to admit I enjoyed that exchange," she said with more than a hint of belligerence. She didn't like dealing with these feelings. The fact she physically reacted to him could easily be explained away. Good grief, she was a normal woman, but to experience this giddy, end-of-the-world sensation wasn't as easily excused.

"You don't have to admit to a damned thing," he answered. He climbed onto the Hog and revved the engine as if he were a participant in the Indy 500.

"Stop," she cried, shouting above the noise. She waved a hand in front of her face to clear away the exhaust so she could breathe.

"What's wrong now?" he snapped, twisting around to look at her.

"Nothing.... Just go slow, all right?"

Separated by only a couple of inches, Meg felt him tense. "I'm not exactly in a slow mood."

"I guessed as much."

She didn't know what he intended as he expertly maneuvered the motorcycle out of her driveway. Mortified, Meg glanced up and down the street, wondering how many of her neighbors had witnessed the exchange between her and Steve.

"Hang on," he shouted.

She placed her hands against his waist in the lightest of holds and was content to keep the contact as impersonal as possible until they turned the first corner. From that moment forward, her arms were wrapped around him tighter than string around a butcher's package.

Meg was forever grateful that he chose not to drive far. He stopped at a park which was less than a mile from her house. After he'd eased into a parking space, he turned off the engine and sat motionless for a couple of moments.

"You all right?" he asked after a while.

"I'm fine. Great.... That was fun." It amazed her the talent she was developing for telling convincing white lies. She was far from fine. Her insides were a mess and it had little to do with the motorcycle ride. Her heart refused to settle down to a normal pace, and she couldn't stop thinking about their kisses. The first time had been traumatic enough, but it didn't compare to her nearly suffocating reaction to his second kiss.

Steve checked his watch. "We'll give it another five minutes and then I'll take you back to the house. That should give Lindsey enough time to worry about you without sending her into a panic."

"Perfect," she said, certain she sounded a little too bright and bubbly.

"Then tomorrow afternoon I'll pick you up after work and you can do your thing to my sister."

Although he couldn't see her, she nodded. Meg only hoped her act for Nancy could be as convincing as Steve's had been with Lindsey.

"After that, there won't be any more reason for us to see each other again," Steve muttered. "As far as I'm concerned, it isn't a minute too soon."

Meg didn't know what she'd done that was so terrible, but she felt much the same way herself. She was just as eager to get him out of her life.

Or was she?

It hadn't turned out to be a good day. Steve would've liked to have blamed his foul mood on work-related problems, but everything at Emerald City Body Shop had run like clockwork. The one excuse that presented itself to him was Meg Remington.

He'd known from the beginning that getting involved with her would mean trouble. Sure enough, he was waist deep in quicksand, and all because he hadn't wanted to hurt the woman's feelings that first night.

That accounted for their dinner date, but thereafter he had no one to blame but himself. Donning his leather jacket and jeans and playing the role of the disgruntled ex-con had been fun. Then he had to get cocky and do something stupid.

The stupid part had come with the kiss. He'd been a fool to force Meg to admit how good it had been.

This was what he got for allowing his pride to stand in the way of reason.

It was her comment about french-kissing her that had got to him. He'd wanted to from the first, and hadn't. The minute she said the words, he knew it was what she'd wanted too. Far be it for him to disappoint a woman.

Well, Steve had learned his lesson. In spades. The next time he was tempted to kiss Meg, he'd go stand in the middle of the freeway. Sweet heaven, the woman could kiss. Only she apparently didn't realize it. Much more of that kissing and he'd have been looking to rent a hotel room.

Not Meg, though. Oh, no. She acted as outraged as a nun. Apparently she'd forgotten that men and women did that sort of thing. Enjoyed it. Looked forward to doing more.

The woman was loony, and the sooner he could extract her from his life, the better. He didn't need this particular kind of hassle. Who the hell did?

One more night, he assured himself. He was taking Meg to meet Nancy this evening, and when they were finished it would be over and they'd never have to see each other again. If she played her cards right. He'd done his part.

Despite his sour mood, Steve grinned. He'd never forget the look of shock and horror in Lindsey's eyes when he walked into her home. The teenager's jaw had nearly hit the carpet when he'd looped his arms around Meg's waist, announced he was an ex-con and Meg was his woman. Lindsey, nothing—he wouldn't forget the look in Meg's eyes, either.

Steve laughed outright.

"Something funny?" Gary Wilcox asked.

Steve glared at his foreman. "Not a damn thing. Now get back to work."

At six o'clock, Steve pulled into the parking space in the alley behind Meg's bookstore. He didn't like the idea of sneaking around and coming to her back door, but that was what Meg wanted and far be it for him to ruffle her feathers. He was well rid of the woman—at least that was what he kept trying to tell himself.

He knocked and waited a couple of minutes, growing impatient.

The door opened and a woman in black mesh nylons and the shortest miniskirt he'd seen in ten years stood in front of him. She vaguely resembled Tina Turner. She certainly had her hair done at the same salon as Tina.

"I'm here for Meg Remington," he said. It irritated him that Meg would make such a fuss about him coming for her at the back of the shop and then send someone else to answer the door.

"Steve," Meg whispered, "it's me."

"What the hell?" He jerked his head back and examined her more thoroughly. "We're going to meet my sister," he reminded her stiffly, "not to some costume party."

"I took my clue from you," she argued. "Good grief. You arrived at my door looking like a member of Hell's Angels—what did you expect me to do?"

Steve rubbed a hand down his face. The hell if he knew anymore. All he wanted was this done and over with. "Fine. Let's get out of here."

"Just a minute. I need to change shoes."

She slipped out of a perfectly fine pair of flats and into spiky high heels that added a good five inches to her stature. Steve didn't know how she managed to walk in those things. She might as well have been on stilts.

He led her around to his car and opened the door. He noticed that she sighed with what sounded like relief when she was inside his car.

"I didn't know what I was going to do if you brought the motorcycle again." In a self-conscious action, she tugged down the miniskirt.

"For the record, I don't often take out the cycle."

She looked relieved, but why it should matter to her one way or the other, he could only speculate.

"Just remember," he said, feeling obliged to caution her. "Nancy's a few years older than Lindsey. She won't be as easily fooled."

"I'll be careful of overkill," she said, "unlike certain people I know."

The drive took an eternity, and it wasn't due to heavy traffic, either. In fact, when Steve looked at his watch he was surprised at what good time they'd made. What made the drive so troublesome—he hated to admit this—was Meg's legs. She'd crossed them, exposing plenty of smooth, lanky thigh. Her high heels dangled from the ends of her toes.

Steve had never considered himself a leg man, or even a breast man. He appreciated women as a whole—some more than others. But it was torture to sit with Meg in the close confines of his car and keep his eyes off her legs. Damn, but the woman was incredible. If only she'd keep her mouth shut!

Nancy stood on the porch when Steve pulled into the driveway.

"This is where your sister lives?" Meg asked.

"It's my home," Steve answered, certain she was about to find some complaint about it.

"Your home?" She sounded surprised. "It's very nice."

"Thanks." He turned off the car engine. "Nancy attends college at the University of Washington nine months out of the year. Our parents retired to Montana a couple of years back."

"I see."

"Does Nancy live with you?"

"Not on your life," he said, and climbed out of the car, "but she found a job here this summer and I agreed to let her stay with me a couple of months. A mistake I don't plan to repeat anytime soon."

Steve was watching his sister for her reaction when he helped Meg out of the car. To her credit, the nineteen-year-old didn't reveal much, but Steve knew his sibling well enough to realize she was shocked by Meg's appearance.

"You must be Nancy," Meg said in a low, sultry voice. She sounded as if she'd developed a raging sore throat in the time it had taken him to come around the front of the car and help her out.

"And you must be Meg," Nancy said, coming down the steps to greet her. "I've been dying to meet you."

"I hope I'm not a disappointment." This was said in a soft, cooing tone, as if she couldn't have borne disillusioning Steve's little sister. She wrapped her hand around Steve's arm and he noticed for the first time that her two-inch nails were painted a brilliant fire engine red.

Ever subtle, Nancy held open the door and smiled in welcome. "Please, come inside."

Meg's high heels clattered against the tile entryway. Steve looked around and was pleased to note that his sister had taken the time to clean up the house a bit.

"Oh, Stevie," Meg whined, "you never told me what a beautiful home you have." She dragged one nail along the underside of his jaw. "But, then, we haven't had time to discuss much of anything, have we?"

"Make yourself comfortable," Steve said and watched as Meg chose to sit on the sofa. She sat and crossed her legs with enough pomp and ceremony for a band to break out in a processional march. She patted the empty space beside her, silently requesting Steve to join her there. He glanced longingly toward his favorite chair, then crossed the room and sat down next to Meg.

The minute he was comfortable, Meg placed her hand possessively on his knee and flexed her nails into his thigh muscle. Then inch by provocative inch she raked her nails up his leg until it was all Steve could do not to pop straight off the sofa. He captured her hand and stopped her from reaching her ultimate destination.

Her look was mildly repentant when she looked at him, but Steve knew her well enough to know the action had been deliberate.

"I thought you might be a bit hungry before Steve takes you to dinner, so I made a few hors d'oeuvres," Nancy said and excused herself.

"What in the hell are you doing?" Steve whispered the minute his sister was out of the room.

"Doing? What do you mean?" The woman had the look of innocence down to an art form.

"Never mind," he muttered from the side of his mouth, as Nancy returned from the kitchen carrying a small silver platter.

"Those look wonderful," Meg said sweetly when his sister placed the tray on the coffee table in front of them. "But I couldn't eat a thing."

To the best of his knowledge it was the first thing his sister had cooked from the moment she'd moved in with him, and he wasn't about to let it go to waste. He opted for a tiny wiener wrapped in some kind of crispy bread dough and popped it into his mouth.

"You shouldn't have gone to all that trouble," Meg told his sister.

Nancy sat across the room from them, and it looked as if she was at a complete loss as to what to say.

"I suspect you're wondering about all those letters I wrote you," Meg said, getting the conversation going. "I hope you aren't unhappy with little old me."

"No, no, not at all," Nancy said, rushing the words together.

"It's just that I've come to know what it is people want from me by the things they say." She turned, and with the tip of her index finger wiped a crumb from the corner of his mouth. Her tongue moistened her lips and Steve's insides turned to mush. Damn, but she could make him want to kiss her.

"I learned a long time ago what men want from a woman," Meg continued after a moment. "It helped when I went to work for the telephone sex lines. Most guys are real sweethearts. They're just looking for a woman to talk dirty to them."

"I see." Nancy's back stiffened and she folded her hands primly in her lap.

"There was always an occasional man who was looking for a good girl to shock, of course. I got real talented at being horrified." She made a soft, gasping sound, then laughed demurely.

"Why... why would someone like you place an ad in Dateline?" Nancy asked and nervously brushed the hair from her face.

"Well, first off," Meg said, holding his sister's gaze, "it's just about the only way someone like me can meet anyone decent. But then, it wasn't your brother who answered the ad, now was it?"

"No, but..."

"Not that it matters," Meg said, cutting her off. "I was tired of my job and all those sort of twisted guys wanting me to say those nasty, nasty things, and I didn't want to start working on my back again."

"On your back," Nancy repeated.

"I'm sorry, sugar pie. I didn't mean to shock you. It's just that I've lived a colorful past—but that doesn't mean that I'm a bad girl. I've got a heart just brimming with love. All I need is the right man." Her gaze wandered to Steve and was long and deliberate. "Your brother's given me a reason to dream again," Meg admitted softly. "Lots of people think women like me don't have feelings, but they're wrong."

"I'm sure that's true," Nancy said.

"I knew I chose right when I learned your brother has his own business."

"He's struggled financially for years," Nancy was quick to tell her. "It's still touch and go. Steve lives one month to the next, isn't that right?" Nancy glared at him pointedly.

"Not any more. I'm more than solvent now," Steve tossed in for good measure, struggling not to laugh. Damn but he was enjoying this.

Meg tightened her arm around his. "I can see how well Stevie's doing for myself. He's wonderful," she said, refusing to drag her gaze from his. Her look of adoration embarrassed him.

"Why, Steve here could make enough money to keep me in the life-style to which I'm accustomed." She laughed coyly.

"Ah..." It sounded to Steve as if his sister was about to start hyperventilating.

"Of course I wouldn't take from him without giving in return. That wouldn't be fair." She snuggled closer to his side and gave him a look so purely sexual Steve was convinced he was about to embarrass them all.

"There are things I could teach your brother," Meg said in a husky, low voice full of sexual innuendo. She looked as if she were eager to get started right that moment and the only thing holding her back was propriety. Her breathing grew labored and her chest rose and swelled gently.

For the life of him, Steve couldn't take his eyes off her chest. To be honest, he'd never paid much attention to Meg's bust. He did now. Her breasts were full and ripe and seemed to be inviting him to sample how lush they'd feel in his hands and mouth.

Soon Steve was having a problem controlling his own breathing.

"Steve," Nancy snapped.

He diverted his attention back to his sister. He stared at her blankly.

"Didn't you hear Meg?" she asked. Her hands were braced against her hips.

He shrugged. Frankly, he knew the two women were conversing, but he hadn't paid attention to their conversation.

"Meg's talking about moving in with you." Nancy took delight in relaying the gist of their chat.

"I don't mean to rush you, dahlin'," Meg whispered, and leaning forward, she licked his earlobe with the tip of her tongue.

Hot sensation shot down his spine.

Meg threw back her head and laughed softly, then whispered just loud enough for Nancy to hear, "I have an incredibly talented tongue."

Nancy closed her eyes as if she couldn't bear to watch any more of this. Frankly, Steve didn't know how much more he could take himself.

"I think it's time we left for dinner," he said. Otherwise he was going to start believing all the promises Meg was making. Heaven knew, he wanted to believe them. The bookseller wasn't anything like he'd assumed. All traces of innocence had disappeared and in their place was the most sexually provocative female he'd ever met. His blood sizzled just being in the same room with her.

"You want to leave already?" Meg gave the impression she was terribly disappointed.

"It's probably for the best," Nancy muttered, and then realizing what she'd said, she hurried to add, "I mean, you two don't want to waste your evening with me, do you?" Her gaze centered on Steve. "You won't be late, will you?"

"No."

"Unfortunately, I'm still working for the phone people," Meg said, "so I won't keep him too long, but I can't promise that he'll have much kick left in him when I'm finished." Thinking herself exceptionally clever, Meg laughed at her own lackluster joke.

It wasn't until they were back in the car and on the freeway that Steve realized how angry he was. It made no sense, but he wasn't rational enough to think matters through just then.

"Why are you so mad?" Meg asked him about halfway back to the bookstore. They hadn't spoken a word from the time they'd left his house.

"Talk about overkill," he muttered.

"I thought I did a good job," she argued.

"You came off like a..."

"I know. That was what I wanted. After meeting me, do you honestly think your sister is going to encourage our relationship?"

"No," he snapped.

"I can guarantee you that Lindsey doesn't want me to see you, either. I thought that was what this scheme of yours was all about."

"It sounded like a good idea at the time," he muttered and tightened his hands against the steering wheel. "It seemed a sure way to convince your daughter that I was the wrong man for you."

"And your sister that I wasn't the right woman for you."

Silence settled over them like nightfall. Neither of them seemed inclined to talk again.

Steve edged his vehicle into the alleyway behind Meg's store and parked his car behind hers.

"I'm not so sure anymore," he muttered, refusing to look at her.

"About what?"

"The two of us. Somewhere in the middle of all this I decided I kind of like you." It hadn't been easy to admit, and he hoped she appreciated what it had cost his pride. "I probably wouldn't have noticed if you hadn't started making yourself out to be something cheap. That isn't you any more than the rebel without a cause is me."

He wished to hell she'd say something. When she did speak, her voice was timid and small. "Then there was the kiss."

"Kisses," he corrected. "And they were damn good and we both know it," he said with confidence. He knew what his own reaction had been, and she hadn't fooled him.

"Yes," she admitted softly.

"Especially the one on the motorcycle," he said, prompting her to continue.

"Especially the one on the motorcycle," she mimicked. "Honestly, Steve, you must have known."

His smile was full blown. "I did."

"I...I didn't do a very good job of disguising what I was feeling."

She hadn't, but then he was in the mood for being gracious.

"How about dinner?" he suggested. He was anxious to have the real Meg Remington back. Anxious to experiment with a few more kisses and see if they were anything close to what his memory kept insisting they had been.

She hesitated. Damn, but the woman had a way of trying his vanity.

"I want to, but I can't."

He bristled and twisted around in the driver's seat in order to face her. "Why not?"

"I promised Lindsey I'd be home by seven and it's nearly that now."

"Call her and tell her you're going out to dinner with me."

She dragged in a deep breath and seemed to hold it. "I can't do that, either."

He didn't understand. "Why not?"

"Following meeting you, I promised her that we'd talk. She wanted to last evening, and we didn't.... That was my fault. You'd insisted on kissing me," she said, blaming him. "And I wasn't in the mood for a heart-to-heart chat with my daughter afterward."

"And it's all my fault?"

"Yes," she insisted.

"Do you know what Lindsey wants to discuss?"

"Of course, I know. You. She isn't keen on me seeing you again, which is exactly the point of the entire charade. Remember?"

"Yeah," Steve said, scowling.

"Are...are you suggesting that you've changed your mind?" she asked timidly.

"Yes." He hated to be the one to say it first, but one of them had to do it. "What about you?"

"I think so."

Steve flattened his hand against the steering wheel. "I swear you're about the worst thing that's ever happened to my ego."

She laughed and leaned her hand against his shoulder. The wig she had on tilted sideways and she righted it. "That does sound terrible, doesn't it?"

He smiled. "Yeah. The least you could do is show some enthusiasm."

"I haven't dated much in the last ten years. But if I was going to choose any man to date, it would be you."

"That's better," he said. Damn, but he wanted to kiss her. One small taste. One small sample. He'd been thinking about doing exactly that from the moment he'd picked her up.

"Only..." Meg said, sounding infinitely sad.

"Only what?" he repeated, lowering his mouth to hers.

Their lips met and it was heaven, just the way he had known it would be. She opened to him the way a flower opens up to sunlight, the way dry ground welcomes rain. She wrapped her arms around his neck and leaned into him, offering him her tongue.

By the time the kiss ended, Steve had propped his head against the window of the car door and kept his eyes closed. It was better than he'd remembered, and that seemed impossible.

Meg's head was against his chest, tucked beneath his chin.

"It's too late," she whispered.

"What's too late?"

"We've gone to a good deal of trouble to convince Lindsey you're the wrong man for me."

"I know, but..."

"Do you think Nancy will believe this was all a silly joke now?"

"No."

"I think it's best to let everything end right here and now, don't you?" she asked.

Steve stiffened. "If that's what you want."

She edged away from him. "I think it might be best," she said, with only a hint of regret.

5

Lindsey was pacing the living room, waiting for Meg, when she walked in the front door.

"Hi, honey," Meg said, striving to sound chipper. She'd led Lindsey to believe she was involved in taking inventory at the bookstore and that was the reason she was so late.

"It's way after seven," her daughter cried, rushing towards her. "You weren't with Steve, were you?"

"Ah..." Meg wasn't willing to lie outright. Half truths and innuendos were about as far as she wanted to stretch this thing.

Lindsey closed her eyes and waved her hands, as if the action would dismiss the question. "Never mind. Don't answer that."

"Honey, what's wrong?" Meg asked as calmly as she could. Unfortunately, she didn't think she sounded all that reassuring. She'd left Steve only moments earlier and already suffered resounding regrets. After following through with this ridiculous charade, Steve wanted to change his mind and continue seeing Meg. She'd quickly put an end to that. Now she wasn't so sure she'd made the right decision.

"Mom," Lindsey said, her dark eyes clear and bright, "we need to talk."

"Of course." Meg walked into the kitchen and reached for the china teapot in the hutch. "My mother always brewed tea when we needed to discuss something important." Somehow drinking tea together helped put everything in perspective. Meg missed those times with her mother.

Lindsey helped her assemble everything they needed and carried it into the formal dining room. Meg poured them each a cup, once the tea had properly steeped. The two sat across from each other at the polished mahogany table.

Meg waited, and when Lindsey wasn't immediately forthcoming she helped get the conversation rolling. "You wanted to talk to me about Steve, right?"

Lindsey's hands cupped the delicate cup and she lowered her gaze. "Do you really, really like him?" How worried and unsure she sounded.

Meg answered before she took time to censor the question. "Yes."

"But why...? I mean, he's nothing like what I thought he'd be." She hesitated. "I suppose this is what Brenda and I get for writing all those letters and pretending we were you. If you'd read his stuff, you would have known from the first what kind of person he really is. At least, that's what Brenda thinks." Having said that, Lindsey clamped her mouth closed.

"Steve is actually a fine person." And he was. The Steve Meg knew, that is.

Lindsey risked a glance at Meg. "You've said a hundred times or more that you don't want me to judge others by outward appearances, but sometimes that's all there is.''

''You're worried about me and Steve, aren't you?'' It hurt Meg to continue with this charade, with her daughter this concerned, but there was no help for it.

Lindsey rubbed her finger along the edge of the teacup. ''I realize now that what Brenda and I did was really stupid. We linked you up with a guy who has a prison record. It was easy to fool us,'' Lindsey said with a scowl, as if she wanted to blame Steve for that as well. ''We're only fifteen years old.''

''But I like Steve, too,'' Meg felt obliged to tell her.

Lindsey looked as if she didn't know how to account for that. ''I'm afraid he's going to hurt you.''

''Steve wouldn't do that,'' Meg assured her, ''but I understand your concern, honey, and I promise you I won't let matters get out of hand.''

Lindsey stiffened her shoulders and blurted out forcefully, as if she'd been holding the words inside and couldn't keep them there any longer, ''I don't want you to see him again.''

''But...''

''I mean it, Mom. This guy is trouble.''

Talk about role reversal!

''I want you to promise me you won't see Steve Conlan again.''

''Lindsey...''

''This is important. You may not understand it now, but I promise you will in the future. There are plenty of other men, law-abiding citizens, who'd give their right arm to know a woman like you.''

Meg resisted sticking her finger in her ear and wiggling it back and forth several times. She couldn't actually be hearing this. The conversation sounded like one she'd had with her own mother as a high school student.

The intense look in Lindsey's eyes softened and she gestured weakly with her hand. "The time will come when you'll thank me for this."

"Really?"

"There'll be a boy in my life that you'll disapprove of and I just won't understand what you see wrong in him," Lindsey continued, more relaxed now. "When that happens I want you to remind me of now."

Meg stared at her daughter, uncertain she should believe what she was hearing. "Are you telling me you'd break up with a boy simply because I didn't like him?"

"No," Lindsey said carefully. "But I'd consider it because I know how I feel about you seeing Steve, and I'd understand how you might feel about someone I was dating. Don't get me wrong," she hurried to add, "I don't dislike Steve.... He really is kind of cute. It's just that I feel you could do a whole lot better."

"I'll think about it," Meg promised.

Lindsey nodded, seemingly satisfied. "I can't ask for anything more than that."

Her daughter had behaved just as Meg had predicted. This was exactly what was supposed to happen. But Meg didn't feel good about it. If anything, she felt more depressed following their conversation than before.

She didn't have any talent when it came to relationships, Meg decided, as she finished up the last of the
dinner dishes later that evening. Steve had come right
out and told her that he'd had a change of heart, and
she'd bungled everything. Instead of admitting that
she felt the same way he did, she'd unmercifully
trampled all over his ego.

Meg glanced toward the kitchen phone. The temptation to contact him was strong. It couldn't end like
this, with them both so uncertain about what they really wanted.

The waiting was terrible. Never had an evening
passed more slowly. It seemed to take Lindsey hours
before she decided to go to bed, and by then Meg was
yawning and tired herself.

As soon as Meg could be reasonably sure that her
daughter was asleep, she tiptoed toward the kitchen
phone and dialed Steve's number. Her heart pounded
until she heard his groggy voice.

"Steve?" she whispered. "Thank goodness it's you.
I didn't know what I was going to do if Nancy answered the phone."

"Meg? Is that you?" He sounded surprised to hear
from her, and none too pleased.

She bristled. "How many other women do you have
phoning you at eleven o'clock at night?"

He didn't answer her right away, and when he spoke
his voice lacked welcome. "I thought you said you
didn't believe it was a good idea for us to see each
other again."

"I . . . I don't know what I want."

"Do you expect me to make your decisions for you?"

"Of course not." This wasn't going well. In fact, it was going very badly. She probably should have waited until she'd had time to think matters through more clearly.

"Is there a reason you called?" he asked gruffly.

"Yes," she answered, regretting now that she'd phoned him. "I wanted to say how sorry I am for being abrupt earlier. I...can see now that I shouldn't have bothered you."

Having said that, she carefully replaced the telephone receiver. For a long moment she stared at the phone, her hand planted over her mouth. It was a gift, Meg decided, a God-given talent she possessed for making herself look foolish.

She turned away, prepared to head up the stairs, when the phone rang, jolting her. Quickly she grabbed it, before the ring woke Lindsey.

"Hello," she whispered.

"Meet me." It was Steve.

"I can't leave Lindsey."

"Why not? She's in bed, isn't she?"

"Yes, but..."

"Leave her a note and tell her you're going to the grocery store."

How reasonable he made it all sound—as if she often did her shopping in the middle of the night.

"She won't even know you're gone," Steve coaxed.

Meg hesitated and closed her eyes. They'd been together only a few hours earlier, and yet it felt as if they'd been apart for weeks.

Her stomach twisted, then quickly—before she could change her mind—she blurted out, "All right, but I can't stay long."

"That sounds fair enough."

They agreed to meet in the Albertson's parking lot. The huge grocery store was open twenty-four hours a day. Meg had been shopping there for years, and since the note she left Lindsey said she was shopping, that was where she intended to be.

She sat in her car until she saw Steve pull into the nearly empty parking lot. Uncertain she was doing the right thing, she climbed out of her vehicle and waited for him.

Steve parked in the spot next to hers. They stood facing each other without speaking.

"I can't believe we're doing this," she whispered.

It appeared she wasn't the only one with doubts. Steve's face was tight and emotionless. "Me either."

By tacit agreement they walked into the store together and each reached for grocery carts. Meg's had a squeaky wheel. The sound vibrated through the canyon of the store, intensifying the annoyance.

The deli was closed, but Steve was able to get them each a cup of coffee from the friendly night manager. They parked their empty carts and sat at a small white table in the deli section. Neither seemed inclined to speak, and Meg guessed it was because they weren't sure what to say.

Certainly, she was at a loss. It encouraged her that Steve had phoned her back, but from his tight, closed features she suspected that he regretted that now.

"You know what you said earlier," she said, broaching the subject of the two of them cautiously.

"I said lots of things earlier. What part are you referring to?"

Meg guessed that was fair. She'd wounded his ego, and he wasn't giving her the chance to do it again. "About the two of us, you know, dating."

"You said Lindsey wanted to talk to you about that."

"She did talk to me," Meg said, "and it was just as I thought. She asked me not to see you again."

His gaze pinned hers. "Did you agree?"

"Not entirely."

The lines around the corners of his eyes crinkled with a frown. "You'd better explain."

"Well, as you've already surmised, Lindsey isn't keen on me seeing you. Which is exactly the reason you stopped by the house, right? She's worried that you're the wrong man for me." It would have helped matters considerably if he hadn't bragged about his prison record and mentioned his parole officer's name at every opportunity. But now didn't seem to be the time to mention that.

"Did you or didn't you promise her you wouldn't see me again?"

"Neither." Meg sipped from the disposable cup and grimaced at the burned taste of coffee.

"Then what did you say to her?"

Meg rolled one shoulder in a halfhearted shrug. "That I'd think about it."

"Have you?"

Propping her elbows against the table's edge, Meg swirled the black liquid around the cup and avoided looking at Steve. "I phoned you, didn't I?"

"I haven't figured out why."

That was the problem: she hadn't, either. "I think you had a point about the two of us continuing to see each other."

"Really?"

Her anger flared. "Would you kindly stop?"

"Stop what?" he asked innocently.

"The next thing I know, you're going to ask me to admit how much I enjoy kissing you."

Steve smiled for the first time. "It wouldn't hurt."

"All right, since it means so much to you, I'll admit it. No man's ever kissed me the way you do. I don't know what to think. I want you to stop, because it feels like my insides are going to burst wide open and at the same time I wish it could go on forever." Having admitted this much, she figured she might as well say it all. "My marriage left me wondering if I was...if I was capable of those kind of feelings...." She paused and lowered her gaze. "I was afraid I was frigid," she admitted in a choked whisper.

Her gaze centered on the coffee, which she sipped as if it were the antidote to a dreaded illness and it was all-important that she drink every last drop.

The last thing she expected her small confession to generate from Steve was a laugh. "You're joking?"

She shook her head forcefully and swallowed at the tightness blocking her throat. "Please, don't laugh."

His hand reached for hers and their fingers entwined. "I wasn't laughing at you, Meg," he said gently. "You're probably one of the most sensual women I've ever met. Trust me, sweetheart, if you're a cold fish than I'm a priest."

Meg looked up and offered him a fragile smile. It astonished her that this man who'd known her for only a short time could chase away the doubts that had hounded her through the years following her divorce.

Steve cleared his throat. "I don't think it's a good idea for you to look at me like that."

"Like what?" she asked, not understanding.

"Like you want me to kiss you right here and now."

Her gaze drifted down. "I guess maybe I do.... That's what makes everything so complicated. I'm strongly attracted to you. It hasn't happened...not ever, not even with my ex-husband, and frankly it frightens the hell out of me."

"I frighten you?" He stood and reached for her hand.

"Where are we going?" she asked.

"Someplace private," he said, looking around the store. He led her through the frozen food section, past the bakery and into a small alcove where the wine was stored. Her back was against domestic beer when he brought her into his arms and crushed her mouth with his.

The kiss was rough with need, but she wasn't sure who needed whom worse. Meg could feel Steve's heart pounding against her breast. She supposed she should have analyzed what it was that attracted them so strongly to each other, but that would have meant clearing her head. Would have meant he had to stop holding her. And Meg didn't want that.

Steve yawned. Damn, but he was tired. With good reason. It had been almost three before he'd gone to bed and four before he'd been able to sleep. His alarm had rung at six.

He arrived at the shop and brewed a pot of coffee. He grumbled a greeting when Gary arrived.

"I certainly hope you're in a better mood than you were yesterday," his foreman told him.

Steve checked over the job orders for the day. "I got woman problems," he muttered as means of an explanation and an apology.

"I should have guessed. What's going on?"

"You don't want to know," he muttered and headed for the garage.

"Sure I do," Gary said, following him. "I don't suppose this has anything to do with Nancy, does it?"

Steve glared at his employee. "What do you know about my sister?"

"Not much," Gary said and held up both hands. "Just what you said about her fixing you up with some woman. It's none of my business, but it seems to me that you and this woman seem to be hitting it off just fine."

Steve glared at the younger man. "What makes you say that?"

Gary laughed and rubbed the side of his jaw. "I haven't seen you this miserable in years. My guess is you're falling in love. Why don't you put yourself out of your misery? Shoot yourself and be done with it."

Steve grumbled and turned away. The kid was a smartass, although now that Steve thought about it Gary might have come up with the perfect solution.

It was noon before Steve had a chance to make it into his office. He made sure no one was looking, when he closed the door and reached for the phone.

A woman named Lois answered at the bookstore. "Is Meg available?" he asked in his best businesslike voice.

"May I ask who's calling?"

Steve hesitated. "Steve Conlan."

"One minute, please."

It took longer than that for Meg to get on the line. "Steve, hi." She sounded tired but happy to hear from him. That helped.

"How are you?" he asked, struggling to hold back a yawn himself.

"Dead. I'm not as young as I used to be."

"Did Lindsey know you'd slipped out of the house?"

"No, but I should never have stayed out that late."

Steve didn't have any argument there. He harbored a few regrets in that category himself. They'd left the Albertson's store when a stock boy stumbled upon them in the wine section, embarrassing Meg no end. Frankly Steve had rather enjoyed the way the color brightened her cheeks.

With little idea of where to take her at that late hour, Steve had driven down to Alki Point, where they sat on the beach in West Seattle and talked.

They hadn't discussed anything earth-shattering, but Steve discovered they shared a good deal in common. Mostly, he discovered that he liked Meg. He was already well aware of what she was capable of doing to him physically. That night, he learned about her as a person.

By unspoken agreement they hadn't kissed again. Steve was convinced they were both forcefully aware of how dangerous kissing had become between them. It wouldn't take much for it to lead to more... a lot more. And when that happened, he didn't plan for it to take place on a public beach.

He didn't know where the time had gone, but the next time he'd looked at his watch he'd been shocked. Meg, too. They'd rushed their farewells without making arrangements to see each other again.

"When can I see you again?" he asked, knowing it was difficult to speak openly while they were on the job.

"I don't know...."

So this was the way it was to be. It seemed they had to start over each and every time they met. "Would you rather we didn't meet again?" he asked.

"You know that isn't true."

"We've got to make some decisions," he said, kicking himself that they'd discussed everything under the moon at the moonlit beach and hadn't come to a single conclusion about what they planned to do with their own relationship.

"I know."

"What about tonight?" he asked.

She hesitated and he gritted his teeth with impatience.

"All right." The longing in her voice was like a healing balm.

"Fine," he said, relieved. "I'll pick you up outside your house at eleven."

"I have to go now."

"Yeah. Me, too."

Steve replaced the receiver and looked up to find Nancy standing in his office doorway, her arms folded, wearing a look of sharp disapproval.

"Was that Meg?" she demanded.

"That's none of your affair," Steve said sharply, resenting her attitude.

"We need to talk about her and I'm tired of you putting me off."

"Meg Remington isn't open for discussion."

"How could you date someone like her?" Nancy asked, her face wrinkled with disgust.

"Might I remind you, you were the one who introduced us?"

"Yes, but she deceived me. Steve, be serious. Can you honestly imagine introducing Meg to Mom and Dad?"

"Yes," he answered calmly.

Nancy threw her arms in the air. "This is your problem, big brother. You're thinking with your pecker again."

"Nancy!"

"It's true. In fact, I'd go so far as to say it's a truth that has plagued men since they were tossed out of the Garden of Eden."

"The Garden of Eden," Steve mused aloud. "A perfect example of a woman messing up a man's life. I think you'd do well to stay out of my business. Understand?"

"But..."

"I make my own decisions," Steve said forcefully.

"And your own mistakes," Nancy muttered, turning around and walking out of the room.

"We're both crazy," Meg said, sitting next to Steve inside his car. She sipped from the can of cold soda, enjoying the sweet taste of it against her tongue.

"Candidates for the loony bin," he agreed.

"I wasn't sure I was going to be able to get away," Meg confessed. "Brenda is spending the night with Lindsey, and those two are sure to be up half the night."

"Did you tell them you were leaving the house?"

"No," she confessed, "but I left them a note. If luck's with me, they won't come downstairs—and if they do, they'll assume I've already gone to bed."

"I was thinking Lindsey and I should have another meeting," Steve said. "Only this time I want you to bring her to the shop. I'll show her around and explain that the whole thing with the leather jacket and the motorcycle was a joke." He waited and then looked to Meg. "What do you think?"

"I'm afraid hell hath no fury like a teenager duped."

"That's what I was afraid you were going to say." Steve finished off the last of his drink and then tucked his arm across her shoulder. "One thing's for sure, I'm through sneaking around in the middle of the night meeting you.''

Meg held the back of her hand to her mouth as she yawned. ''Frankly, I'm too old for this.''

''You and me both,'' he muttered.

Meg finished her soda and, twisting, leaned back against Steve, his chest supporting her back. She dared not close her eyes for fear she'd soon be asleep.

''Nancy isn't any too keen on me seeing you, either.''

''I'll talk to her, explain everything.'' It amazed Meg that she could sound so confident, as if all she needed to do was look the teenager in the eye, laugh and explain it had all been one big joke. Only, like Lindsey, Meg suspected Steve's sister wouldn't laugh.

''It's settled, then,'' Steve said. ''I'll talk to Lindsey and you'll talk to Nancy. Neither one of them is going to enjoy being the butt of a joke, but it wasn't like we planned this. Besides, it serves them right for the way they manipulated us into meeting.''

''One would think they'd be pleased,'' Meg inserted. ''Their plan worked—not the way they wanted, but we're dating each other and that's what they wanted. Right?''

Steve chuckled and rubbed his chin along the crown of her head. ''Right.''

Steve sighed and the breath seemed to come deep from inside his chest. It was as if it flowed through him like water slipping over a waterfall.

''I wish it wasn't like this,'' Meg whispered.

Steve kissed the top of her head. ''So do I.''

Meg smiled and twisted around in his arms so that they faced each other.

Steve nudged the hair from her temple and his hands lingered at her face. His mouth was so close she could feel his breath brush her cheek. A shiver of awareness skidded down her arms.

Meg closed her eyes and lifted her mouth to Steve's, silently asking him to kiss her. She noticed that he hesitated for a fraction of a second, as if he experienced second thoughts about what might happen.

Meg was well aware of the temptation they were under, but she didn't care. Nothing was important but the feel of this man making love to her, this man kissing her as if she were more precious than gold.

His kiss was warm and gentle, sweet and tender. But his gentleness didn't last long. There was a hunger in Steve, a hunger in Meg that flared to life like a torch dipped in gasoline. Soon his hands cupped Meg's breasts and she was making soft sounds deep inside her throat.

"Meg..." He sounded as if he were being tortured.

"I know...I know."

His hands were inside her sweater, fiddling with the clasp of her bra and not having much luck. "I'm far too old and particular to make love in the front seat of a car."

She smiled, then claimed his lower lip between her teeth and sucked gently.

"Maybe I'm not as old as I thought," Steve amended.

"We'd better stop," she said with a good deal of reluctance.

"I know." But his hands remained where they were, his palms filled with the weight of her breasts. Steve braced his forehead against hers. "Tomorrow," he said and drew in a deep, even breath.

"Tomorrow," she repeated, but she hadn't a clue what she was agreeing to. She opened her eyes and leaned back. "What about tomorrow?"

"We'll talk to Lindsey and Nancy."

"Good idea."

Fifteen minutes later Steve dropped her off at her house.

It wasn't until Steve drove away that she realized she'd left her purse in his car. Her purse had the key to her house.

"Damn," she muttered to herself and wandered around the backyard, hoping Lindsey had forgotten to lock the sliding glass door. It was locked.

No help for it—she searched until she found the spare key, expertly hidden under the flowerpot on the porch. It had been there for so many years she wasn't sure it would work.

Luckily it did. Being as quiet as she could, Meg slipped into the house.

Meg climbed the stairs and silently tiptoed into her room. She undressed without turning on the light and was in bed only minutes after she'd left Steve.

The neighbor's German shepherd barked in the distance and Lindsey looked up from painting her toenails. "There it is again," she said.

"I thought I heard something, too," Brenda said.

"Wolf doesn't normally bark without a reason."

Ever curious, Brenda walked over to the bedroom window and peered into the backyard below. After a moment, she whirled around. "There's someone in your backyard," Brenda whispered, wide-eyed.

"This isn't the time for jokes," Lindsey said, continuing to paint her toenails a bright shade of pink. "We were discussing my mother, remember?"

Brenda didn't move away from the window. "There is someone there."

"Who?"

"It's a man.... Oh my goodness, it is a man. Come and look."

The panic in her friend's voice was enough to catapult Lindsey off the carpet. Walking on her heels in order to keep her freshly painted toenails as far off the carpet as possible, she hobbled toward the window.

Lindsey's heart was lodged in her throat when she recognized the dark form. "It's Steve Conlan," she whispered.

"Oh my goodness. What's that in his hand?"

Lindsey focused her attention on the object Steve carried. It looked like a purse. Gasping, she twisted away from the window and planted her back against the wall. She gestured wildly toward the portable phone.

"What's wrong?" Brenda cried. "Are you having an asthma attack?"

Lindsey shook her head forcefully. "He broke inside the house and stole my mother's purse." Brenda handed her the phone and Lindsey dialed 911 as fast as her nervous fingers could manage.

She barely gave the operator time to answer. "There's a man in our backyard," she whispered frantically into the mouthpiece. "He took my mother's purse."

The emergency operator seemed to have a thousand silly questions she wanted Lindsey to answer. Lindsey did the best she could.

"He's a convicted felon.... I can give you the name of his probation officer if you want. Just hurry," she pleaded.

"Officers have been dispatched."

"Please, please hurry." Lindsey was convinced unless the police arrived within the next minute or two Steve would make a clean getaway.

Steve debated whether he should leave Meg's purse on the front porch or not. It would be easy enough to tuck it inside the milk box, but she'd never think to look there.

He walked around the house to the backyard, thinking there might be someplace there he might put it where she'd find it first thing in the morning.

There wasn't.

The only thing he'd managed to arouse was the neighbor's dog. He would have rung the doorbell and handed her the silly thing if there'd been any lights on, but she'd apparently gone to bed. He wasn't especially eager to confront Lindsey, either. Not yet.

He still hadn't made up his mind, when he heard a noise from behind him.

"Freeze."

Steve didn't know who the hell was talking to him, but whoever it was sounded serious.

"Put the purse down on the ground and very carefully turn around."

Once more Steve did as instructed. With his arms raised high over his head, he slowly turned around to find two police officers with their weapons drawn and pointed at him.

"It looks like we caught ourselves a burglar."

6

— ▸ ◂ —

"If you'd let me explain," Steve said, squinting against the light at the two police officers. A dog barked ferociously in the next-door neighbor's yard.

"Do you always carry a woman's purse around with you?"

"It belongs to..."

"My mother."

Although Steve couldn't clearly see her face, he recognized the righteous tones as belonging to Meg's daughter. Lindsey and her friend stood beside the two law-enforcement officers and looked as if they'd gladly have provided the rope for a hanging. Lindsey stood with her arms akimbo like a warlord, eager for battle.

"Wolf." One word from the second girl silenced the neighbor's German shepherd.

"My name's Steve Conlan," Steve said, striving to come across as sane and reasonable. This was, after all, merely a misunderstanding.

"I wouldn't believe him if I were you," Lindsey advised the officers. Then in lower tones she added,

"He has a criminal record. I happen to know for a fact that he's a convicted felon."

"I'm not a felon," Steve growled. "Officers, if you'd give me the opportunity to explain . . ."

"His parole officer's name is Earl Markum." Lindsey cut him off, her voice raised and indignant. "He told me so himself."

"I know Earl Markum," the younger of the two policemen said. "And he is a parole officer."

"I know him, too," Steve barked impatiently. "We went to high school together."

"That's a likely story if I ever heard one."

The inflection in Lindsey's young voice reminded Steve of Meg when she was furious with him. Like mother, like daughter, it seemed.

"If you'd let me explain," Steve tried again, struggling to keep calm. It wasn't easy when two six-shooters were aimed at his midsection and a couple of teenage girls were accusing him of only God knew what.

"Don't listen to him," the other teenager instructed. "He lies real good. He had us believing all sorts of things that weren't true, and all because he thought we were Lindsey's mother."

A short silence followed her announcement. "Say that again?" the older officer inquired.

"How well do you know this man?"

"My name's Steve Conlan," Steve tried again.

"Which may or may not be his real name." This, too, came from Lindsey's friend.

"If you'll let me get my wallet, I'll prove who I am," Steve assured them. He strove to sound vaguely amused by the dispute. He lowered his arms a bit and started to move his hand around his backside.

"Keep your hands up and where I can see them."

"What's going on down there?" The voice drifted down from the upstairs area of the house. A sweetly feminine, slightly groggy voice.

Steve glanced up, and to his great relief discovered Meg's sweet face softly framed in the window behind a mesh screen. The moonlight illuminated that portion of the house so that it was almost as bright as day.

"Meg," Steve shouted, grateful she'd heard the commotion. "Kindly tell these men who I am, so they can put their weapons away."

"Steve?" she cried, shocked. "What are you doing at my house at this time of the night?"

"Do you know this man?" The law-enforcement official asked, tilting his head back and shouting to Meg.

"Ma'am, would you mind stepping outside," the second officer instructed. He mumbled something Steve couldn't hear under his breath.

"I'll be right down," Meg told them, and Steve watched her turn away from the window.

"Have you been sneaking around seeing my mother?"

"Lindsey, it's not like it sounds," Steve said, experiencing a twinge of guilt for the way he'd misled the girl. He had planned on talking to Meg's daughter at his earliest convenience, but he hadn't intended to do it in front of the police.

"I'd be more interested in why he has your mother's purse, if I were you," the second teenager whispered.

"I already know why he's got Mom's purse," Lindsey said loudly. "It's perfectly obvious he stole it."

Steve rolled his eyes. "For the love of heaven, I was trying to return it."

"You have my purse?" This came from Meg.

Steve relaxed and lowered his arms. "You left it in my car," he explained.

"Thank goodness you found it." Meg, at least, displayed the appropriate amount of appreciation. "I didn't know how I was going to get it back."

Now that the flashlight wasn't glaring in his eyes and the officers had returned the guns to their holsters, Steve saw Meg for the first time. In fact, he couldn't take his eyes off her. She wore cotton baby-doll pajamas that revealed a length of sleek, smooth thigh. The short top—what there was of it—silhouetted her lush breasts, which seemed to bulge through the paper-thin material.

Steve feared he wasn't the only one who'd noticed Meg's attire—or rather lack of it—either. Both police officers were gazing approvingly in her direction. Steve was about to ask the younger of the two to wipe the grin off his face, but he held his breath and counted backward from ten.

He got to five. "Lindsey, go get your mother a robe."

"I don't have to take orders from you," snapped the teenage girl.

Meg blinked and seemed to realize for the first time that she wasn't exactly dressed for a church outing. She folded her arms as if she'd developed a sudden chill, but all that did was bunch up her breasts even more, until they threatened to spill out of the top.

In an apparent effort to divert a shouting match one officer asked Lindsey a few questions, while the other engaged Steve and Meg in conversation.

"You know this man?" he asked Meg.

"Yes, of course. His name's Steve Conlan."

"Steve Conlan." The officer made note of it on a small pad.

"He didn't steal my purse, either."

Steve cast the other man an I-told-you-so look, but said nothing.

"You went out with Steve behind my back?" Lindsey cried, looking around the broad shoulders of the policeman. Her narrowed eyes centered disbelievingly on Meg. "I can't believe you'd do something like that...after our talk and everything."

Meg cast a guilty look downward. "We'll discuss all this later."

It was apparent Lindsey wouldn't be easily dissuaded. "After our talk, I really thought I was getting through to you. Now I see how wrong I was to think we could communicate on an adult level."

"If you'd give me a chance to explain..." Steve said, wanting to smooth the waters between the two.

Static from the intercom the police officer carried was followed by a muffled voice. Steve only managed to make out a couple of words, but apparently the two men were able to decipher the message.

"Is everything under control here?" the policeman asked Meg.

"It's fine."

"Young lady?"

Lindsey folded her arms and pointed her nose toward the night sky. "All I can say is that my mother's a sorry disappointment to me."

"I'm afraid I can't help you there, miss."

"I didn't think you could," the teenager said, with an air of defeat. "I thought better of her than to date a man of such low moral fiber."

"Lindsey!"

"Why don't we all go inside and talk this over," Steve suggested. He felt more than a little ridiculous standing in Meg's side yard, and frankly he was eager to clear the air between himself and Lindsey.

"I have nothing to say to either of you," Lindsey said and with a good deal of ceremony she marched into the house, with Brenda scurrying behind her.

Steve watched the two parade single file around the side of the building and released a deep breath. He was about to apologize for having made such a mess of things, when Meg whirled around to face him.

"I can't believe you!"

Steve ran his fingers through his hair. Meg didn't seem to appreciate that this ordeal hadn't been a Sunday school picnic for him either.

"I apologize, Meg." He did feel badly about all the trouble, but he'd only been trying to help. When he'd found her purse, returning it had seemed the best thing to do. He didn't want her wondering where it was, and he'd honestly thought he could do it without starting another world war.

"How dare you ask my daughter to get me a robe."

Steve's head jerked up. His throat tightened and nearly closed with the strength of his anger. "I damn near got myself arrested—with no help from your daughter, I might add—and you're upset because I happen to object to you traipsing around in front of the entire neighborhood wearing a Band-Aid."

Meg opened and closed her mouth a number of times.

"Okay, it's a little more than a Band-Aid," he amended, "but not much more. Neither one of those law-enforcement officers could take their eyes off your breasts. I supposed you enjoyed the attention."

"Don't be ridiculous. I came downstairs as fast as I could, in order to help you."

"You call parading in front of those men half naked helping me? All I needed or wanted was for you to identify me so I could leave. That's all." Each word grew louder and more intense. He was close to losing his cool and he knew it.

"I think you'd better go," Meg said, pointing in the direction of the street, in case he didn't know the way. Steve noticed, with satisfaction, the way the tip of her index finger wobbled.

"I'm out of here," he assured her, "and not a minute too soon. You might have appreciated the embarrassment and trouble I endured for you, but I can see that you don't. Which is fine by me. Just fine and dandy."

"You don't think you didn't embarrass me?" she shouted.

"You weren't the one who had a gun pointed at you and a teenager claiming you were a menace to society."

"Lindsey was only repeating what you'd told her." Meg pushed the hair away from her face, using both hands. "This isn't working."

"Wrong," he countered sharply. "It's working all too well. You make me crazy, and I don't like it. I don't like it one damn bit.

"If I'm going to get arrested, I want it to be for someone who's willing to acknowledge the trouble I've gone through for her." Certain he was making no sense whatsoever, Steve stalked toward his car and drove away.

Meg squared her shoulders and wrapped her tattered mantle of pride around her shoulders as she opened the screen door and walked back into the house. The exhaust from Steve's car lingered in the yard, a reminder of how angry he had been when he left her.

She was angry, too, and confused.

It didn't help matters to find Lindsey and Brenda sitting in the darkened living room waiting for her.

"You should both be in bed," Meg told the two.

"We want to talk to you first," Lindsey announced and folded her hands together on her knees. Her gaze narrowed as Meg stepped into the room.

"Not tonight. I'm tired and upset."

"You!" Lindsey cried. "Brenda and I are exhausted, but none of that matters. What does is that you broke your word."

"I didn't promise not to see Steve again," Meg reminded the girl. She'd been careful about that.

Meg went back to the door and stood in front of the screen door, half hoping Steve would return. Not knowing what she'd say or do if he did.

"What did you do? Sneak out of the house to see him?"

Meg lifted one shoulder in a half answer.

"You did!" Lindsey was outraged. "When? Tonight?"

Meg lifted the other shoulder.

"Can't I trust you any longer?"

"Lindsey, Steve's not exactly what he led you to believe."

"I'll just bet," she said in a huff. "He's got you hoodwinked, hasn't he? You'd believe anything he says, because that's what you want to believe. You're so crazy about this guy you can't even see what's right in front of your face."

If she'd been a little less upset herself, Meg might have been willing to set the record straight right then and there. "We want to talk to you," Meg told her daughter. "Steve and I together, and explain everything."

"Never!"

"Mrs. Remington, don't let him fool you," Brenda threw in dramatically.

"Let's not worry about all this now," she said as the defeat settled over her. "It's late and I have to be to work early in the morning."

Lindsey stood, her hands knotted into fists at her sides. "I want you to promise me you won't see him again."

"Lindsey, please."

"If you don't, Mom, I won't have any choice but to restrict you for the rest of your life."

"It's time we had a little talk," Nancy said, delivering a steaming cup of coffee to the breakfast table. After the night he'd had, the last thing Steve wanted was a tête-à-tête with his troublesome younger sister.

"No thanks," he mumbled.

Nancy left the table, taking the coffee with her.

"I want the coffee."

"Oh." She brought it back and slipped into the chair across from him. "Something's troubling you."

"Little gets past you, does it?" He damn near scalded his mouth in his eagerness to get some caffeine into his bloodstream.

"Can you tell me what's wrong?" She stared at him with big brown eyes that suggested she was the answer to all his concerns, if only he'd let her help him.

"No."

"It has to do with that Meg, doesn't it?"

Once more Steve made a noncommittal reply. He didn't care to discuss Meg Remington just then. What he'd told her was right on target. She made him crazy. No woman had ever affected him as powerfully as she did. After the way they'd parted, he didn't know if they'd see each other again, and damn it all, that wasn't what he wanted.

"She's not the woman for you," Nancy said, her eyes as solemn as a judge's.

"Nancy," he said tightly, "don't say anything more. Okay?"

She bunched her fists together and closed her eyes. "I knew it. You're falling in love with her."

"I'm not, either," he muttered. Hugging the mug with both hands, he tried the coffee a second time, sipping from the edge in an effort to keep from burning his mouth.

"Thou protesteth too much," she told him, with a sanctimonious sigh. "I'm afraid you've made it necessary for me to take matters into my own hands. I didn't want to have to do this, but I don't have any choice. Someone's got to look out for your best interests."

Steve lowered the mug to the table and glared at his sister through narrowed eyes. "What did you do this time?"

"Nothing yet. There's this woman, a widow I met on campus, and I'd like you to get to know her. She's nothing like Meg, but as far as I'm concerned . . ."

"No." He wasn't listening. Not to another word. The last time his sister had roped him into her schemes he'd met up with a crazy woman with a loony daughter. No more.

"But Steve."

"You heard me." The chair made a scraping sound against the tile floor as he stood. "I won't be home for dinner."

Nancy stood, too. "What time will you be back?"

Steve regarded her suspiciously. "I don't know. Why?"

"Because the least you can do is meet Sandy."

Steve clenched his teeth. "You invited her to the house?"

"Don't worry—I didn't mention you. I wanted the two of you to meet casually. She's nervous, just yet, about dating again, and I was afraid if I told her about my big, bad brother she'd turn and run in the opposite direction."

"That sounds like what I intend to do. If you want to work on anyone's love life, you might try your own."

"All right, all right," Nancy said, sounding appropriately defeated. "Just stay away from Meg, all right? The woman's bad news."

Steve's short laugh lacked humor. "You're telling me?"

A week passed, and Steve refused to dwell on his confrontation with Meg. He didn't contact her and she didn't phone him.

He hated like hell to end it all, but frankly he wasn't willing to apologize. And he doubted that she was, either. He didn't know where that left them.

Damn, if he didn't miss her. He tried to tell himself otherwise. Tried to convince himself a man has his pride. Tried not to think about her.

And failed.

Early one afternoon, out of the blue, Nancy stopped by the shop with a friend. The pair were on their way to play tennis, or so Nancy claimed.

Nancy smiled a little-sister smile and cheerfully asked if Steve would give Sandy an estimate to repair her fender.

Sandy was a petite thing. Cute and pixielike. There was a fragile air to her, and he remembered his sister mentioning she was a widow.

It didn't take Steve long to figure out that this Sandy was probably the same one Nancy was so keen on him dating. The woman who would save him from Meg's clenches.

"I'm pleased to meet you," Steve said, wiping the grease from his hands on the pink cloth he had tucked in his hip pocket.

Nancy smiled innocently, looking pleased with herself.

"I'll have a written estimate for you by the time you two return from your tennis match."

"You won't have to work late again, will you?" Nancy asked, not even attempting to be coy.

Steve could already see what was coming. His conniving sister was about to wrangle a dinner invitation out of him. One in which he'd be stuck entertaining the young widow.

"I'm afraid I'm tied up this evening," he said stiffly.

"Oh, darn. I was hoping you could take me and Sandy to dinner."

"I can't," he said, diverting his attention away from the two women. "Now, if you'll excuse me."

"It was a pleasure to meet you, Mr. Conlan."

"The pleasure was mine," he said and turned away.

Unfortunately, it didn't end with Sandy. His sister had several more friends with dented fenders, who needed estimates, in the days that followed.

"The next time a woman comes in and asks for me, I'm unavailable. Understand?" he told his crew. Steve made certain that on her next pop-in visit Nancy would know he didn't have time for her matchmaking games.

"I was only trying to help."

"Thanks, but no thanks." He sat at his desk, making his way through the piles of paperwork stacked in front of him.

Nancy expelled a belabored sigh. "You aren't seeing Meg again, are you?"

His hand tightened around the pen. "That's none of your damned business."

"Yes, it is. A woman like that could ruin your life."

In some ways she already had, but Nancy wouldn't understand that. Every time he met another woman, Steve found himself comparing her to Meg. Invariably everyone else fell short. Far short. He was miserable without her and killing himself in an effort to convince himself otherwise.

Nancy left, and Steve leaned back in his chair and studied the phone. All it would take was one phone call. He wouldn't even have to mention the incident with the police and her purse. He could even make a joke of it and buy her a pair of flannel pajamas. The kind that went all the way from her feet to her neck.

They'd both laugh, say how sorry they were and put an end to this silliness.

Then he'd take her in his arms, hold her and kiss her. This was the part his mind dwelled on most. The phone nearly hypnotized him.

"Steve." Gary Wilcox stuck his head in the office door.

Steve jerked his attention away from the telephone.

"There's someone here to talk to you. A woman."

Impatience caused Steve's blood to boil. "What did I say earlier? I gave specific instructions for you to tell any more of my sister's friends that I'm unavailable."

"But, boss..."

"Is that so difficult to understand?"

"Nope," Gary said without emotion. "If that's what you really want. I don't have a problem doing that, if that's what you really want, but I kinda had the feeling this one is special."

Knowing his foreman had cast an appreciative eye toward the widow lady, Steve strongly suspected it was Sandy who'd dropped by unannounced. "You talk to her."

"Me?"

"Yeah, you."

"What am I supposed to say?"

Steve rubbed a hand down his tired face. Was he going to have to do everything himself? "I don't know, just say whatever seems appropriate. I promise you Nancy won't be sending any more eligible women into the shop."

"Nancy didn't send this one."

The pen slipped free from Steve's hands and rolled across the top of the desk. "Who did?"

"She didn't rightly say. All I got was her name. Meg Remington. I seem to recall hearing it mentioned a time or two, generally when you were upset about something."

Steve scooted back the chair and slowly stood. His heart reacted with a furious, swift pace. "Meg's here?"

"That's what I've been trying to tell you for the last five minutes."

Steve sank back onto the wooden chair, his heart so light he felt like singing. "Send her in."

A mischievous grin slow danced across Gary's mouth. "That's what I thought you'd say."

Steve stood, then sat back down again and busied himself with a number of things on his desk. He wanted Meg to think he was busy. The minute she walked into the room, he'd set everything aside. Yes, what he did was important, but she was more so.

A full five minutes passed and still she didn't come. Steve came out of his office and ran into Gary who frowned and shook his head. "She left."

"Left?"

Gary nodded. "That's the only thing I can figure out. She must have overheard you say that you were unavailable and slipped away then."

Steve muttered a four-letter word and hurried out of the shop. He wasn't sure where he'd find her, but he wasn't going to let her walk out of his life. Not again.

It wasn't until it was nearly seven that he gave up and drove to her house. That he was willing to confront her dragon of a daughter was a sign of how desperate he'd become.

He stood outside on her front porch and rang the doorbell. Waiting for someone to answer, he buried his hands in his pockets. A protective device, he realized, to keep from reaching for her the instant she appeared.

"One minute." He heard her call from the other side of the doorway.

It didn't take nearly that long before the thick door opened and Meg's gaze slammed into his.

His gaze drifted over her, slowly, heatedly. He'd wanted to play it cool, casually mention he was in the neighborhood and heard she'd stopped by the office. Their eyes held each other and Steve hadn't a prayer of hiding his feelings. She wore a pretty pale blue summer dress.

"Hello, Steve."

"Hello."

The screen door stood between them.

They stared at each other and he lowered his gaze to her lips and swallowed.

"Can I come in?" he asked. Pride be damned. It had been cold comfort in the past two weeks. If he had to apologize, then so be it. He wanted her back in his life.

"Of course." She unlatched the door and pushed it open.

Steve stepped inside. Emotion thickened the air until Steve could barely breathe or think properly. Lugging her into his arms didn't seem appropriate just then, but that was all he could think to do. It didn't

help that her nipples had hardened and showed
through the thin material of her dress.

"Where's Lindsey?"

Meg's answer was breathy and uneven. "She's out
for the evening."

He desperately needed to touch her. Reaching up, he
cupped her cheek in his rough palm. Slowly, Meg
closed her eyes. She leaned her head into his hand and
bit into her lower lip.

"I had to come," he whispered.

"I'm so sorry."

"Me, too." They were a pair of fools.

Unable to wait a second longer, Steve wrapped her
in his arms and brought her mouth to his. Gentleness
was beyond him, his hunger as great as any he'd ever
known.

Meg clenched his shirt as if she needed an anchor,
something to secure her during the wild, sensual
storm. His tongue sought out every part of her mouth
as he backed her against the door. It clicked closed and
his hands were at her hips, rubbing her buttocks, urging her closer, dragging her against his swelling heat.

Meg gasped, and Steve didn't know if it was from
pleasure or pain. Fearing the force of his desire might
hurt her, he dredged up the will to drag his mouth
from hers. With his hands framing her cheeks, he
studied her beautiful face. Her shoulders heaved, and
he realized his own breathing was equally labored.

"I hurt you?"

"No...no," she whispered hurriedly to assure him.

He rubbed the pad of his thumb across her moist, swollen lips. The action was unhurried—an apology for his roughness, his eagerness.

She moaned softly and he kissed her again. Gently. With restraint. Her arms were around his neck, and Steve had never tasted a kiss more sweet.

"I was going to phone," he told her, burying his face in the gentle slope of her neck. "A thousand times I told myself I would call. Every minute apart was torture."

"I wanted to phone you, too."

"So damn proud."

"You were right," Meg confessed. "I should have been wearing a robe."

"I was jealous, pure and simple." He felt her smile against the side of his face and he smiled.

"I would have been, too.... I am."

"I'll have you know I didn't date a single one of the women Nancy arranged for me to meet."

Meg jerked back. "What women?"

"Ah...it's not important."

"It is to me."

It would have been to him, as well, and so he explained briefly. "Nancy felt it was necessary to save me from the clenches of a loose woman, so she introduced me to a number of her school friends."

"And you refused." Meg sounded pleased.

"I wanted to talk to Lindsey. Explain."

"Me, too. But we can't now."

"So I see."

"Hold me," she said, nestling into his arms. "I don't want you to leave for a very long time."

Steve planted tiny kisses along the side of her neck, marking his way back to her lips. When he kissed her again, his tongue made in-and-out movements reminiscent of lovemaking. He knew what was on his mind, and he sincerely hoped Meg was thinking along those same lines.

"How long will Lindsey be gone?" he whispered into her ear. He'd wanted to sit down and talk with the teenager, but if she was away that couldn't be helped.

Meg stilled. "She's staying the night with Brenda."

His hold tightened. "Meg," he said, and kissed her with a hunger he couldn't deny. He brushed the hair out of her face. "I want to make love to you. I never pretended otherwise. I realize there's a lot of things we need to clear up between us before we make that kind of physical commitment, but there's no better time than the present."

He kissed her again, greedily, pacing himself. "Thank God you stopped by the office. I don't know how long it would have taken me to come to my senses otherwise."

"Come to your office," Meg said, breaking away from him. "I was never at your office."

7

←—→

"It doesn't matter if you were at my office or not," Steve said, kissing Meg slowly. Thoroughly.

His mouth covered hers and she couldn't find so much as token resistance, although her mind swirled with multiple questions.

Heaven help her, she was starved for the taste of him. Starved with the need to have him hold her, love her. The loneliness had been suffocating. Before she'd met Steve, her life had seemed just fine. Then within a matter of weeks she realized how empty everything seemed without him.

"I've missed you so much," she told him between deep, drugged kisses.

"Me, too."

"You should have phoned," she chastised, and kissed him back.

"You, too."

"I know. I know."

"I'm crazy for you." The strength of his desire bulged against her abdomen, reminding her of how close they were to throwing caution to the wind and making love. If ever the time was right it was now, with Lindsey gone for the night.

But...

The questions returned—new ones that had nothing to do with his claim that she had been at his office. There'd only been one man in her life, Lindsey's father, and by the time they'd divorced Meg had felt a failure as a wife. Inadequate. Frigid. Unresponsive. She couldn't bear to have Steve discover how inept she was as a woman.

"Steve...Steve." Her fingers were imbedded in Steve's hair as his mouth roamed over her throat. She had to make him stop, make him understand. "Stop, please."

He went stock-still, his lips pressed against the hollow of her throat. His breathing was hard and uneven. "You want me to stop? Now?"

"Please...for just a moment." It was difficult to catch her own breath. Her breasts tingled and molten desire coiled in the pit of her belly, but she couldn't allow him to continue, knowing what would happen if she did. "Did you say you thought I'd been to your office?"

"That's what Gary told me." He lifted his head, his eyes cloudy with passion. "It doesn't matter—I'm here now. I've missed you so damned much. I can't believe either one of us let this go on so long."

"But it does matter," she argued, though not too strenuously. "I wasn't there."

Steve shut his eyes, and he seemed to be fighting something within himself. After several moments, he straightened and gently eased away from her. She felt chilled outside his arms. Cold and alone. The feeling wasn't unlike what she'd experienced the past two weeks without him.

"I'm glad you're here," she whispered. "So very glad. I've missed you, too. It's just that before we..." She was certain her face was as red as a ripe tomato. How she wished she was more sophisticated about these matters. "You know."

"Make love," he finished for her.

"Yes... We should come to some sort of under- standing. I'm doing a poor job of this.... It's just that I think we should talk first, don't you?"

"Come here," Steve said, taking her by the hand. He led her into the living room, looked around and then chose the big overstuffed chair that was her fa- vorite.

He sat, and reaching up, pulled her down onto his lap. "So you think we should talk first?"

"Yes," she said, hating the way her voice trem- bled.

"I agree, but first I want to clear the air. You say you didn't stop by my office this afternoon?"

"No. I was at the store until after six." Then, be- cause she was afraid he would think she was trying to save face, she added, "You can check with Lois if you want."

Steve frowned. "I believe you. Why shouldn't I?" His hands framed her face and his gaze studied her. "But that isn't the reason you stopped us just now, is it?"

Meg lowered her gaze. "No," she whispered.

"I thought not. Are you going to tell me, or do I have to torture it out of you?"

"Tell you what?" Steve's arm went around her waist. It felt good to be this close to him.

He ceremoniously unfastened the button at the top of her dress. "You're going to seriously disappoint me if you're wearing a bra."

Meg giggled. "I'm wearing a bra."

He groaned. "The way I figure it, your reluctance has something to do with your marriage."

"My marriage?" Before she could respond one way or another, he had the next three buttons undone. His fingers fumbled with the clasp of her bra, and with some effort he managed to work it free. Her bounty spilled free into his waiting palm.

"It doesn't take a detective to figure out that your ex-husband badly hurt you."

"No divorce is easy," Meg admitted, "but I'm not an emotional cripple, if that's what you mean."

"It isn't." Steve lifted her breast and her rigid tip stood proudly at attention. He moaned and gently brought the peaked softness into his mouth. His tongue swirled around the rigid tip, shooting shivers of desire up and down her back. Meg gnawed on her bottom lip as Steve took the nipple into his hot mouth and sucked gently.

She arched her back to offer him more. More of her breast. More of herself. More of her heart.

"Steve . . . oh, please."

When she was certain she couldn't bear any more of the hot sensation, he released her breast and buried his face in the valley between. They were starved for each other, too hungry to carry on a serious conversation.

"I can't seem to keep my hands off you," he said between gritted teeth. "I wanted to talk to you about your marriage. Instead, I'm a hair's space from ravishing you."

And she was a hair's space from letting him.

"It was a friendly divorce," Meg insisted, but none too strenuously. He'd taken the fight out of her.

Steve eyed her suspiciously. "From what I've seen, divorces generally start out that way."

"It was different with Dave and me," she insisted, striving to keep her breathing even.

"How's that?"

Meg didn't want to rehash her dead marriage. Not now. "We parted amicably."

"What caused the divorce?"

Meg closed her eyes and sighed deeply. "He had a cupcake on the side," she said, making sure none of her bitterness leaked into her words. For years she'd kept the feelings of hurt and betrayal buried.

In the beginning, it had been for Lindsey's sake. Later, she was afraid to face the anger for fear of what it would do to her. "Dave didn't love me any longer," she said, as if it hadn't been a concern to her one way or the other.

"What about Lindsey?"

"He knew I'd always be there for her, and I will. He lives in California now."

"What about his commitment to you and Lindsey?"

"I don't know—you'll need to ask Dave about that."

"How long did this business with Cupcake go on before he told you?"

"I haven't a clue." She had her suspicions, plenty of those, but none she was willing to discuss with Steve. "I do know that by the time Dave got around to telling me he wanted a divorce, Cupcake was pregnant."

"In other words, there wasn't anything you could do but step aside, or so you felt?"

"I had no problem doing that." Maybe if she'd loved Dave more, she would have been willing to fight to save her marriage. But by the time Dave told her about Sandy, she wanted out of the relationship. Out of the marriage. Just plain out.

"So you divorced."

"Yes, with hardly a fuss. He gave me what I wanted."

"And what was that?"

"He was willing to let me raise Lindsey." She exhaled sharply. "It's not what you're thinking." Meg didn't know why she was so insistent.

"And what am I thinking?"

She smiled and placed the back of her hand against her forehead and put on a forlorn look. "That the divorce traumatized me."

"I wasn't thinking that at all," he assured her. "The marriage had already taken care of that."

Meg dropped her hand and battled the tears that leaked to the surface. How well Steve understood.

"It wasn't enough that your husband had an affair. When he walked out on you and Lindsey, the son-of-a-bitch made damn sure you carried the blame for his lack of faithfulness, didn't he?" When she didn't respond, he asked her a second time, his voice gentle. "Didn't he?"

Meg jerked her head away for fear he'd read the truth in her eyes. "It's over now.... It was a long time ago."

"But it isn't over. If it was, we'd be upstairs making love instead of sitting here. You've never been able to trust another man since Dave."

"No," she whispered, her head lowered.

"Oh, baby," he said tenderly, gathering her in his arms. "I can't say that I blame you."

She blinked rapidly in an effort to forestall the tears. "I trust you," she told him, and she knew instinctively that Steve would never walk away from his family.

"You do trust me," he said, "otherwise you wouldn't let me this close to you. Just be warned, I intend to get a whole lot closer, and soon."

With anyone else Meg would have felt threatened, but with Steve it was more of a promise. One she was eager to have him fulfill.

"It's better that we wait to make love," he surprised her by adding.

"It is?" Her head shot up.

"I want to clear the air with Lindsey first," he told her. "Get matters settled between us, once and for all. I'd much rather be her friend than her foe." His hands worked at refastening her bra, but he had a far more difficult time getting it back together than he had had undoing it.

In the end, Meg assisted him. And teased him. Kissing him, using her tongue in the erotic ways he had taught her.

It was a long time before her dress was fastened. A very long time.

"Just exactly where are we going?" Lindsey asked for the second time, staring out the car window.

"I already told you." Meg was fast losing patience with her daughter.

"To see Steve at work?"

"Yes."

"Work release, you mean."

"Lindsey," Meg said emphatically. She'd never known the teenager to be more difficult. "Steve owns his own business. We both thought if you could see him in action, then you'd know that what he told you about being an ex-con was all a farce."

Lindsey remained sullen for several minutes, then asked, "Why'd he say all those things if they weren't true?"

Her daughter had a valid point, Meg wouldn't argue with her there, but they'd gone over this same ground ten times or more. "We wanted you to dislike him."

Unfortunately Steve's plan had worked all too well. Apparently, Meg had done an equally good job with Nancy, because his sister wasn't keen on him continuing to date her, either. What a mess they'd created.

"Why wouldn't Steve want me to like him?" Lindsey asked stiffly.

"It's a long story," Meg said, "and one I'm not especially proud of."

Lindsey's shoulders heaved. "Is this another one of those you-can-lift-the-suitcase-when-you're-big-enough lessons?"

"No, it's an embarrassment I don't want to rehash just now. Okay?"

"I guess," Lindsey pouted.

Meg pulled into the parking lot at Steve's business and watched as Lindsey's gaze took in everything around the well-established body shop.

There were three large bays all filled with vehicles in various forms of disrepair. A number of men dressed in blue-striped coveralls worked over the cars.

"They all look like they came straight from a prison yard," Lindsey mumbled under her breath.

"Lindsey," Meg pleaded, wanting this meeting to go well. "Promise me you'll at least give Steve a chance."

"I did once, and according to you he lied."

Once more, Meg had no argument. "Just listen to him, okay?"

"All right, but I'm not making any promises."

The shop smelled of a mixture of paint and grease; the scents weren't unpleasant. There was a small waiting area with coffeepot, paper cups and several outdated magazines.

"Hello," Meg said to the man standing behind the counter. "I'm Meg Remington. I believe Steve is expecting me."

The man studied her. "You're Meg Remington?" he asked.

"Yes."

"You don't look anything like the Meg Remington that was in here last week."

"I beg your pardon?"

"Never mind, Gary," Steve said, walking out from the office. He smiled warmly when he saw Meg. Lindsey sat in the waiting area, reading a two-year-old issue of *Car and Driver* as if it contained the answers to life's most complicated questions.

"Hello, Lindsey," Steve said.

"Hello," the teenager returned in starched tones.

"Would you and your mother care to come into my office?"

The teenager stood. "Will we be safe?"

A hint of a smile cracked open Steve's mouth, but otherwise he didn't let on that her question had amused him. "I don't think there'll be a problem."

"All right, since you insist." She set aside the magazine and stood.

Steve ushered them into the spotlessly clean office and motioned for them to sit in two chairs on the other side of his desk.

"Would you like something to drink?" he asked.

"No, thanks."

Meg couldn't remember when Lindsey had been less friendly to anyone. It wasn't like her daughter to behave this way, unless she thought she was protecting her mother.

"I have a confession to make," Steve said, after an awkward moment. He leaned back in his chair.

"Shouldn't you be telling this to the police?" Lindsey asked.

"Not this time." His eyes connected with Meg's. She tried to tell him how sorry she was, but nothing she'd said had changed Lindsey's attitude.

"I did something I deeply regret," Steve continued undaunted. "I lied to you. And as often happens when someone lies, it comes back to haunt him."

"I'm afraid I was a party to this falsehood myself," Meg added, wanting Lindsey to know Steve wasn't the only one at fault.

"How do you know it's really a lie?" Lindsey demanded of Meg. "Steve could actually be a felon. He might be sitting behind a fancy desk and everything, but who's to know if what he says is true even now?

"Who are you really, Steve Conlan?" Lindsey demanded, leaning forward and planting her hands on the edge of his desk. One would think she was interrogating him for the FBI.

"I'm exactly what I appear. I'm thirty-five years old, a bachelor. I own this shop, and have ten full-time employees."

"Can you prove it?"

"Of course."

A knock sounded against the door.

"Come in," Steve called.

The man who had greeted her when she first arrived stuck his head inside the door. He looked around and smiled apologetically. "Sorry to interrupt, but Sandy Janick's on the phone."

Steve's brow folded together in a frown. "Gary, this is Meg Remington and her daughter, Lindsey."

Gary smiled and nodded in their direction.

"Are we working on Sandy's vehicle?" Steve wanted to know. "I don't remember the name on a work order."

"No, she's the widow friend your sister was trying to set you up with. Remember?"

"Tell her I'll call her back," Steve said without hesitating.

Meg bristled. A tingling numbness settled around the area of her heart. He'd admitted that his sister had been playing the matchmaker role. So Nancy had set him up with a widow. Probably one without a troublesome teenager and a bunch of emotional garbage she was dragging around from a previous marriage. Meg swallowed at the hard lump forming in her throat.

"Gary," Steve said, stopping the other man from leaving. "Will you kindly tell Lindsey who owns this shop?"

"Sure," the other man said with a wide grin. "Mostly the IRS."

"I'm serious," Steve said, impatiently.

Gary chuckled. "Last I heard it was Walter Milton at Key Bank. Oops, there goes the phone again." He was gone an instant later.

"Walter Milton." It certainly didn't take Lindsey long to pick up on that. "So the truth is out. You really don't own this business."

"Walter Milton's my banker and a good friend."

"So is Earl Markum, your parole officer," Lindsey mumbled, looking bored. "I'm afraid I can't believe you, Mr. Conlan. If you were looking to get me to change my mind about you seeing my mother, it didn't work." Then turning to Meg, she added, "I wouldn't trust him if I were you. He's got the look."

"The look?" Meg and Steve asked simultaneously.

"Yup. I've seen his face before, and my guess was that it was in some post office."

Meg ground her teeth with frustration. "Lindsey, would you kindly stop being so difficult."

"I don't think it's a good idea for you to date a man who lies."

"You're right," Steve surprised them both by saying. "I should never have made up that ridiculous story about being a felon. I've learned my lesson and I won't pull that stunt again. All I'm asking is that you give me a second chance to prove myself."

"I don't think so."

Meg resisted tossing her arms in the air. She'd never seen Lindsey behave like this.

"You know what really irritates me?" Lindsey said. "It's that you'd involve my mother in this scam of yours. That's really low."

"I don't blame you for being angry with me," Steve said, after a moment. "But don't be upset with your mother—it was my idea not hers."

"My mother wouldn't stoop to anything that underhanded on her own."

Meg's eyes connected with Steve's and she wanted to weep with frustration.

"I was hoping that you'd find it in your heart to forgive me," Steve said contritely, returning his attention to Lindsey.

"I suppose I could," she said magnanimously.

Steve relaxed enough to smile. "I'd like for us to be friends."

"Sure, but this doesn't mean that I approve of you seeing my mother."

"But, Lindsey," Meg pleaded.

"Mom, we can't trust this guy. We already know how willing he is to lie. And what about that phone call just now," she said, wagging her index finger at Steve. "Another woman calls, and you know she doesn't have car parts on her mind, and he can hardly wait to get back to her. You saw the look in his eyes as well as me."

"Don't be ridiculous," Steve snapped. "I'm crazy about your mother. I wouldn't hurt her for the world."

"That's what they all say."

"I think you'd better go wait in the car," Meg suggested.

Lindsey eagerly shot out of the chair and rushed from the office, leaving Steve and Meg alone.

"I'm so sorry," she whispered, standing.

"I'll try to talk to her again," Steve said, walking around the desk and pulling her into his arms. "All she needs is a little time. Eventually, she'll learn to trust me." He raised her hands to his mouth and kissed her knuckles. "One thing's for certain, though...."

"What's that?"

"I'm through sneaking around meeting you. I'm taking you to dinner tonight and I'm coming to the front door. Lindsey will just have to accept the fact we're dating. I'll ask her if she'd like to join us."

"She won't," Meg said with certainty.

"I'm still going to ask. She may not accept me now, but in time I'll win her heart just the way I intend to win her mother's."

What Steve didn't seem to understand was that he already possessed hers.

At seven, Meg was humming softly to herself and dabbing perfume on the pulse points behind her ear and at her wrist. Steve was due to arrive any minute for their dinner date.

The telephone rang, but Meg didn't bother to answer it. There wasn't any need. Lindsey raced at breakneck speed for the phone, as if her reaching it before the second ring was all that kept the world safe from destruction.

"Mom." Her name screeched from the kitchen downstairs, reached her in the master bath.

"I'll be right there," she called back, taking her time to check her reflection in the bathroom mirror one last time.

Lindsey yelled something else with less enthusiasm, which Meg couldn't hear.

"Who is it?" Meg asked, coming out of her bedroom.

"I already told you it's Steve," Lindsey said indifferently as she passed her on her way out of the kitchen.

Meg glanced at her watch and hurried down the stairs. She removed her earring and reached for the phone. "Hello."

"Hi," he said, sounding discouraged. "Listen, sweetheart, I ran into a little bit of a problem and it looks like I'm going to be late."

"What kind of problem?" It was already later than when she normally ate dinner, and frankly Meg was hungry.

"I'm not sure yet. Sandy Janick phoned and apparently she's got a flat tire. . . ."

"Listen," Meg said with feigned cheerfulness, "why don't we cancel dinner for this evening? It sounds like you've got your hands full."

"Yes, but . . ."

"Frankly I'm hungry right now. It isn't any big deal—we'll have dinner another night."

Steve hesitated. "You're sure?"

"Positive." She was trembling so badly it was difficult to remain standing. Steve and Sandy. No doubt Nancy had arranged the flat tire, but if Steve couldn't see through that, then it was obvious that he wanted to spend time with the other woman. "It's not a problem," Meg insisted.

"I'll give you a call tomorrow."

"Sure. . . . That would be great," she said. She barely heard the rest of the conversation. His voice droned on and Meg hoped she made the appropriate responses. She must have, because a couple of moments later the line was disconnected.

Closing her eyes, Meg exhaled and replaced the receiver.

"Mom?"

Meg turned around and faced her daughter.

"Is everything all right?"

She nodded, unable to chase away the numb feelings that attacked the pit of her stomach and radiated out like a burning pain.

"Then how come you're so pale all at once?"

"I'm fine, honey. Steve and I won't be going out to dinner after all." She tried to sound as if nothing was amiss, but it felt as if her entire world was collapsing in around her. "Why don't we order a pizza? You can phone, if you like.... Order whatever you want. Okay?"

She was overreacting and knew it. If Steve was doing something underhanded, he wouldn't tell her that he was meeting Sandy Janick. He'd do the same things Dave had done. He'd lie and cheat.

"I'm going upstairs to change clothes," Meg said and blindly headed for the stairs.

She half expected Lindsey to follow her and decree she'd been right all along. Steve wasn't to be trusted. But to Meg's amazement, her daughter said nothing.

"I knew if anyone could help Sandy with this flat tire it would be you," Nancy said, smiling benevolently toward her older brother.

Steve glanced at his watch, frustrated and angry with himself. His sister had done it again. She'd manipulated him into doing something he didn't want to do. Instead of spending the evening with Meg the way he'd intended, he'd been trapped into helping the two out of a fix.

Leave it to his sister. Not only had Nancy and Sandy managed to get a flat tire, but they'd been on the Mercer Island floating bridge in the middle of rush-hour traffic. Steve had to get a tow truck and then meet them at his shop. From there they'd all ended up back at the house, and Sandy had let it be known that she was looking for a little male companionship. There was a time when Steve would have leapt at the chance to console the attractive widow. But no longer.

"I can't tell you how much I appreciate your help," Sandy told him.

"No problem." Pointedly he looked at his watch. It was still early enough for him to steal away and visit Meg. Lindsey was certain to disapprove of him stopping by after nine, but that couldn't be helped.

The teenager was proving to be more of a problem than Steve had anticipated. The girl was downright stubborn. Well, she was dealing with a pro, and Steve wasn't about to give up on either one of the Remington women. Not without one hell of a fight.

"You're leaving?" Nancy asked as Steve headed for the front door.

"Yes," he said. "Is that a problem?"

"Not really." His sister wore a downtrodden look, as if he'd deeply disappointed her.

"I have to be going myself," Sandy Janick told him. "I really can't thank you enough."

"No problem." She was a gentle soul and Steve wished her well, but he wasn't interested in becoming her knight in shining armor. Not when there were two other damsels whose interest he coveted.

Nancy leapt up from the table and followed him. "Where are you headed?" she asked.

Steve stopped and glared at her. "What makes you think it's any of your business?" he asked in a heated whisper.

"Because I have the feeling you're off to see that . . . that floozy."

Steve gritted his teeth. "Meg is no floozy. She owns a bookstore."

"That's not what she told me."

"Listen. I'm thirty-five years old and I won't have my little sister running my love life. Now I helped you and your friend, but I had to break a dinner date with Meg to do it."

"Then I'm glad Sandy got that flat tire."

Steve had had enough. "Stay out of my life, Nancy. I'm warning you."

His sister's shoulders moved up and down as if she'd come to some momentous decision. "I'm afraid I can't do that. I'm really sorry, Steve."

"What do you mean, you can't?"

"I can't idly stand by and watch the brother I've always loved and admired make a complete fool of himself. Especially when it's over a woman of ill repute."

Steve's patience was gone. Vanished. What they should do was put his sister and Meg's daughter in a room and let the two of them slug it out.

"I won't let you do this," Nancy insisted. She planted herself in front of the door, her arms spread-eagled across the thick frame.

The phone rang just then, and Steve knew he was saved. Nancy flew across the room and leapt for the telephone.

Hoping to make a clean getaway, Steve opened the door and walked outside. As he suspected would happen, Nancy tore out after him a couple of moments later.

"It's for you," she called from the front porch.

Steve was already in his car and he wasn't willing to be waylaid by his sister a second time.

"Tell whoever it is, I'll call them back."

"It's a woman."

Steve hesitated. "What's her name?"

"Lindsey," she called at the top of her voice. "And she wants to talk to you."

8

→ ←

The last person Steve thought to hear from was Meg's standoffish teenage daughter. He climbed out of his car and took the porch steps two at a time. He walked directly past his sister and without speaking a word headed straight toward the phone.

"Lindsey? What's the problem?" he asked. He was in no mood for games and he wanted it known. If Meg's fifteen-year-old thought she had him by the tail, she was wrong.

"Are you alone?" Lindsey asked him.

Steve noticed that her voice was considerably lower than normal. If he was making a guess, it would be that Meg knew nothing about her daughter's call.

"My sister's here," he answered glancing toward Nancy who stood with her arms folded, glaring at him with unconcealed disapproval.

"Anyone else?" Lindsey asked and then with a snide tone of voice added, "Especially someone named Sandy."

It sounded as if Lindsey was possessive, which was ridiculous. The kid would be glad for an excuse to be rid of him. "No. Sandy left a few minutes ago."

"So you were with her," she accused, her voice elevating slightly.

In light of the confrontation with his sister, Steve's hold on his patience was already strained. "I take it there's a reason for your call?"

"Of course," Lindsey muttered with an undignified huff. "I want to know what you said that upset my mother."

"What I said?" Steve didn't understand.

"After your phone call, she told me to order pizza for dinner, and then she said I could have anything on it that I wanted. She knows I like anchovies and she can't stand 'em. Then," Lindsey said, after a short pause, "the pizza came and she looked at me like she didn't have a clue where it came from. Something's wrong and I want to know what it is."

Steve scratched his head. "I don't have a clue."

"Mom's just not herself. I think you'd better come over and talk some sense into her."

An invitation from the veritable dragon of a daughter herself. This was a stroke of luck Steve hadn't expected. "You sure you can trust me?"

"Not really," she said with feeling. "But I don't think I have a choice. My mom's keen on you. In light of how fickle you've turned out to be, I can't figure it. But then I never could see what she thought was so great about you in the first place."

The kid was a definite hazard to his ego, but Steve was willing to let her latest comment pass.

"You think your mother's upset because I broke our dinner date?" he asked. "Well, I've got news for you—she was the one who called it off. She said it was no big deal."

"And you believed her?"

"Shouldn't I?"

Steve could picture the teenager rolling her eyes. "Either you aren't nearly as smart as you look, or you've been holed up in prison for so long you don't know anything about women."

Steve didn't find either choice especially flattering. "All I did was phone to tell her I was going to be a few minutes late. What's so awful about that?"

"You were late because you were meeting another woman!"

"Wrong," Steve protested, having a difficult time holding on to his patience. "I was helping another woman. Actually two women, one of whom was my sister."

"Don't you see? My dad left my mother because of another woman. He made up all these lies about where he was and what he was doing so he could be with her."

"And you're worried that your mother assumes I'm doing the same thing? Lindsey, really, isn't that a bit of a stretch?"

"Yes . . . no. I don't know," the teenager said, sounding uncertain. "All I know is you canceled . . ."

"She canceled."

"Your dinner date because you were meeting another woman. . . ."

"Helping another woman and my sister."

"Whatever. All I know is that mom hasn't been the same since, and if you care about her the way you keep saying..."

"I do."

"Then I suggest you get over here, and fast."

He was about to tell her that he had been on his way when he'd been so rudely interrupted, but before he could open his mouth the line was disconnected.

Steve stared at the receiver, shook his head and replaced it.

"What's wrong with Meg?" Nancy asked, standing just inside the living room.

Steve shook his head. "The hell if I know. No one ever told me falling in love would be so damned complicated." Having said that, he marched out the door.

Nancy raced after him. "You're in love with her?"

"You're damn right."

A huge smile lit up his sister's face. Steve stood next to his car and stared, wondering if he was seeing things. A smile was the last reaction he would have expected out of her.

Steve muttered to himself on the short drive between their houses. He didn't stop muttering until he rang the doorbell.

The door was opened less than two seconds later by Lindsey. "It took you long enough," she said in a huff.

"Lindsey, who is it?" Meg asked, stepping out from the kitchen. She had apparently been doing dishes, because she had a dish towel and a coffee mug in her hand. "Steve," she whispered, "what are you doing here?"

"Have you had dinner yet?"

"Not really," Lindsey answered for her mother. "She nibbled on a slice of pizza, but that was only so I wouldn't bug her. I ordered her favorite kind, too," she paused and grimaced. "Vegetarian."

"Weren't you hungry?" Steve asked, silencing Lindsey with a look before she could answer on her mother's behalf.

Meg shook her head. "Not really. What about you . . . ? Did you get anything to eat?"

"Nope."

"There's leftover pizza, if you're interested."

"I'm interested," he said, and stepped toward her. But it wasn't so much the pizza as the woman who concerned him. Lindsey was right—Meg looked as if she'd been stewing all evening.

"You're not going to eat, are you?" Lindsey demanded.

"Why not?" Steve asked.

The teenager slapped her hands against her sides. "What my mother really needs is reassurance. If you had a romantic thought in that empty space between your ears, you'd take her in your arms and kiss her."

All Steve could do was stand and stare. This was the same pesky adolescent who had been a source of constant irritation from the moment they'd met. Something had changed, and he didn't know why.

"Lindsey?" It appeared Meg was having the same questions as Steve. They both stared, with their mouths hanging open, at the teenager.

"What?" Lindsey demanded. "Oh, you want to know about my abrupt change of heart. Well, I've been thinking. If Steve really meant what he said about the two of us learning to be friends, then I guess I'm willing to make an effort." This was said as if it had come at great personal sacrifice. "Actually, I can't see any way around it. It's clear to me my mother has fallen in love with you."

"Lindsey!"

Steve enjoyed the way the color heated up Meg's pale cheeks.

"And it's equally clear to me that Steve must care just as deeply about you, especially if he was willing to put up with all of my insults. Frankly, I can't see fighting it any longer. It would only be an exercise in frustration. And really I can't be expected to keep a constant eye on you two. I do have my own life."

Lindsey's change of heart was welcome news to Steve. The kid held the all-important key to Meg's heart and he knew it. He'd never win her heart, if he didn't gain Lindsey's approval first.

"Don't get the idea I like any of this," Lindsey added—just to be on the safe side, he guessed. "But I can learn to live with it."

"Great," Steve said, and offered the teenager his hand. "Then, let's shake on it."

Lindsey studied his hand as if she wasn't sure she wanted to touch him. Once she had made the decision, he noticed that her shake was firm and confident.

"You are nothing like what you were supposed to be," she muttered under her breath.

"I apologize for being such a sorry disappointment," he said out of the corner of his mouth.

"That can't be helped now. Mom's crazy about you."

"I think she's pretty neat herself."

Lindsey rolled her eyes. "So I noticed."

"What's going on with you two?" Meg asked.

"Nothing," Lindsey answered, and the lone word oozed with innocence. She looked at Steve and winked.

He returned the gesture, pleased to be on solid ground with the teenager. "Did someone say something about pizza?"

"I did," Meg told him. "Come into the kitchen and I'll heat up the leftovers."

"Mother," Lindsey groaned and regarded her parent with a look of intense disappointment. "I thought I could at least count on you to be a little more romantic. It's plain to me that I'm going to have to do everything myself."

"What did I do wrong now?"

"Couldn't you hand-feed Steve something?"

Meg took some time to think this over. "I've got leftover chicken I could make into a salad. If he doesn't like that, there's always peanut-butter-and-jelly sandwiches."

"I'd rather have the pizza." Steve interjected before he found himself tied to a chair being hand-fed in the name of some romantic fantasy.

Before Lindsey could protest, Steve followed Meg into the kitchen. "Do you know what she's talking about?"

Meg smiled and opened the oven door. "I haven't got a clue." She took out the pizza box and set it on the counter.

Steve climbed onto the stool and asked, "What happened earlier?"

Meg hesitated, licking the cheese off the end of her fingers. "I suppose Lindsey phoned you?"

"Yes, but I was on my way over here, anyway."

He noticed that her gaze avoided his, as she made busywork of setting two huge slices of pizza on a plate and heating them inside the microwave. "After your phone call, I had a bit of a panic attack."

"About?" he prompted.

"You.... Us."

"And?" She certainly didn't seem to be forthcoming with information.

"And I worked it out myself, and felt foolish afterward. You aren't the same kind of man Dave was...is. If you phone to say you're helping another woman, then that's exactly what you're doing."

"You thought I was seeing someone else?" Clearly the woman had no concept of how smitten he was with her. He hadn't looked at another woman cross-eyed or any other whichway from the moment they'd met.

"I feel like a fool now," she said, setting the sizzling pizza slices in front of him. She propped her elbows on the counter and buried her chin in her palms. "It was as if the craziness of my marriage was back. You see, at one time I opted to believe Dave. He'd make up the most ridiculous stories to account for the huge gaps of time he was away from home, and I'd believe him." She paused and shrugged. "I guess because I wanted to so badly. But Dave's no longer my problem.''

"A leopard doesn't change his spots," Steve said, finishing off the first slice. "If Dave cheated on you, then it'll only be a matter of time before he cheats on his present wife. It only stands to reason."

"I know so. From what Lindsey said after her visit to California this spring, Dave's marriage is on shaky ground. I'm sorry for him and for his wife."

The low strains of a soulful violin drifted toward them. Steve glanced at Meg and she shrugged and looked perplexed.

Lindsey appeared in the kitchen just then, looking thoroughly disgusted. "It's clear to me you two need my help."

"Help?" Steve repeated. "With what?"

"Romance." She walked into the room and claimed Steve's hand and then her mother's and led them both into the living room. The furniture had been pushed to one side and the lights turned down low. Two crystal glasses and a bottle of red wine sat ready to be put to good use.

"Now, I'll disappear into my room for a little while," she said, "and you two can do all the things I've read about in novels."

Steve and Meg looked blankly at each other.

"Don't tell me you need help with that, too?"

"We can take it from here," Steve was quick to assure her.

"I should hope so," Lindsey muttered, and with an air of superiority headed up the stairs.

The music was low and sultry. Inviting and intriguing. The same way the woman who stood no more than a few inches from Steve enticed and fascinated him.

Once the teenager was out of sight, Steve held his arms open to Meg. "Shall we dance?"

Steve could have sworn she blushed, very prettily too, before she slipped into his embrace. He brought her close and sighed, involuntarily, at how incredibly good it felt to hold her.

"I'm not very good at dancing," she complained.

"Not to worry. All we need do is shift our feet a little." He laid his cheek next to hers, and for the sake of romance closed his eyes.

Romance.

He hadn't the time or the patience for such rot. Or so he'd believed. Then he'd met Meg and his organized, safe, secure world had been tipped upside down. Nothing had been the same since, and Steve strongly suspected it never would be again.

Even Gary Wilcox seemed to appreciate the difference between Steve's attitude toward Meg and his attitude regarding the other women he'd dated over the years. Steve didn't know how his foreman had figured it out, but he had. Of course, inviting Meg and Lindsey to the shop might have given Gary a clue. Having Lindsey see him in action had been an excuse and Steve knew it. He was looking to impress Meg, show her he was successful. Prove to her that he was worthy of her attention.

Steve liked to keep his personal life separate from the business. His personal life—that was a joke. He'd worked years, dedicating his life to building the body shop into a thriving business. He'd been successful, but that success had come at a price. There was damn little space left in his life for love.

But there was room for Meg and Lindsey. His heart felt as if it were about to explode, it was so full.

Unfortunately, his heart wasn't the only thing threatening to explode. Meg's lithe body moved with the music provocatively, seductively against his. Her thighs rubbed against his thighs. Her marvelous full breasts all but seared holes in his chest. She was soft in all the right places and he was hard—and growing harder.

Rock hard.

They stopped moving, the pretense of dancing more than he could sustain any longer. He braced his legs in such way that they formed a cradle and then he dragged the lower portion of her body against the considerable bulge in his jeans.

Meg sighed and raised her head so their eyes met in the dim light. "See what you do to me," he told her softly. "Wanting you this much is downright embarrassing."

"Unfortunately, you can't know all the things you do to me." She lowered her gaze. "I want you too.... It frightens me how much."

"You can always tell me." He lowered his head so she could whisper it in his ear.

"I can't."

"Then show me," he urged. He ran his long fingers up through her hair and held his breath as he slowly lowered his mouth to her.

Meg opened to him the way a water lily welcomes the rain, holding back nothing. Their tongues mated in an ancient ritual of need. Her response was as fierce and strong as his own. Whatever restraint he'd felt in her before was gone. She gave herself to him wholly completely.

"Oh, Meg," he rasped and kissed her again, unable to taste enough of her.

The sound of someone clearing her throat made it through the thick fog of desire and permeated his brain.

Lindsey. Again.

Steve groaned inwardly. Slowly, with heavy reluctance, he loosened his grip on Meg and eased his body away from hers. The cost of pulling away from her warmth was close to pain.

She resisted. "Don't stop."

"Lindsey's back," he whispered.

Meg groaned and buried her face in his sweater.

"Hello, again," Lindsey said cheerfully from the staircase. "It looks like I returned in the nick of time." She pranced down the stairs, walked over to the wine bottle and sadly shook her head. "How disappointing, you didn't even open the wine."

"We didn't get a chance," Steve muttered disparagingly.

"I gave you twenty minutes," she argued. "From what I can see that was about five minutes longer than I should have waited. You're a fast worker."

"Lindsey," Meg said, in what Steve was certain was meant to be her sternest voice. Unfortunately, she sounded like a frog with a sore throat.

"I know I'm making a pest of myself—and I apologize, I really do. But we've been talking in my sex-education class about a lot of important subjects, and there's a case to be made for abstinence."

"What's that got to do with your mother and me?" Steve made the mistake of asking.

"You don't really want me to answer that, do you?" Lindsey asked. "Mom's flustered enough as it is."

"I guess not."

"We could discuss safe sex, if you want."

Steve watched as Meg's face turned a deep shade of lobster red. "Lindsey!" This time her mother's voice was loud and clear. "You're embarrassing me."

"Sorry, Mom, but I figured the time to raise the subject is now instead of later," the teenager said and plopped herself down on the sofa. She reached for the wine bottle and examined the label. "It's a good month, too. September. Brenda's uncle bought it for us. He said it wasn't a great wine, but it'd get the job done."

Steve's hand gripped Meg's shoulder. "It was thoughtful of you to think of it."

"Thanks." She smiled broadly. "But we were going for the romantic element."

"Now," Steve said, "would you mind very much if your mother and I talked? We didn't get much of a chance to do that earlier."

"I suppose that would be all right . . . only I need to know something first." She set the wine bottle back down and looked intently toward Steve. "Are you going to marry my mother or not?"

Meg made a small mewling noise that sounded as if she was mortified beyond words. She sank onto the ottoman and covered her face with both hands.

"Well, are you?" Lindsey pressed, ignoring her mother entirely.

Steve couldn't very well say he hadn't been thinking along those lines, because little else had been on his mind for the past several days. He was in love with Meg. When he wasn't with her, it felt as if there was a giant hole in his life. In his heart. Lindsey was as gutsy as all get-out, but he enjoyed her, too.

Steve had never imagined himself with a ready-made family, but he couldn't see himself without Meg and Lindsey. Not now.

"I believe that's a subject your mother and I need to discuss privately, but since you asked I'll tell you."

Lindsey scooted toward the edge of her seat and Meg dropped her hands and looked up at him as if she half expected something unexpected to happen.

"You're going to marry us, aren't you." Lindsey's words were more statement than question. A satisfied smile lit up her face. "You're really going to do it."

"If your mother will have me."

"She will, trust me," Lindsey answered, looking gleeful. "I've known my mother a good long time and I've never seen her this googoo-eyed over a man. She's nutso over you."

"I can do my own talking, thank you very much," Meg said sternly. "This is the most humiliating moment of my life—no thanks to you, Lindsey Marie Remington." She stood and braced her hands against her hips. "Go to your room and we'll talk when I've finished begging Steve to forgive you."

"What did I do that was so terrible?" Lindsey demanded.

Meg pointed the way to the stairs, and Steve noted that her index finger wobbled dramatically.

It looked for a moment as if Lindsey was about to argue, then apparently she thought better of it. Her shoulders slumped forward and she moved with excruciating slowness toward the stairs.

"All I was doing was helping," she muttered under her breath.

"We'll talk about that later, young lady."

Lindsey's deep blue eyes met Steve's as she passed him. "I know I'm in deep yogurt when she calls me young lady. She's mad. Be careful what you say, okay? Don't ruin everything now."

"I'll try my best," Steve promised out of the side of his mouth.

Meg waited until her daughter had reached the top of the staircase before she spoke. "I can't begin to tell you how deeply sorry I am for that little exchange." Although her voice was calm and even, Steve wasn't fooled. Meg was angry.

"I'll have Lindsey apologize after I've had a chance to cool down myself. I dare not speak to her now." She paced the carpet, her steps fast-paced and jerky. "I want you to know I absolve you from everything that was said."

Steve rubbed his jaw, not sure he followed her gist. "Absolve me from everything that was said?"

"Yes," she returned heatedly. "I want it understood right here and now that I don't expect you to marry me."

"But I kind of like the idea."

"I don't," she flared. "Not when my daughter's the one who practically ordered you to propose. Now please, I think it might be best if you left."

Steve tried to protest, but Meg ushered him to the door and he could see now wasn't the time to try to reason with her.

"I've never been more mortified in my life," Meg told Lois. She mentally counted the change and placed it inside the cash register. The store was due to open in ten minutes and she'd never felt less ready to deal with customers.

"But he said he wanted to marry you, didn't he?"

"It was a pity proposal. Good grief, what else could he say?"

Lois restocked the front slots with the latest best-sellers. "Steve doesn't look to me like the kind of guy who'd propose marriage if he didn't mean it."

"He didn't mean it."

"What makes you so sure?"

Meg wanted to find a hole, crawl inside and hide for the rest of her natural life. No one seemed to appreciate the extent of her humiliation. Certainly, Steve hadn't. He'd tried to hide it from her, but he'd viewed the incident with Lindsey as one big joke.

She wouldn't have mentioned it to anyone. Lois knew because she sensed something was wrong with

Meg the minute she arrived for work. In a moment of weakness, Meg had blurted out the entire episode.

"Have you explained to Lindsey what she did?" Lois asked.

"In this frame of mind," Meg told her, "I thought it better not to try. I'll talk to her when I can do so without weeping with frustration."

"What I don't understand," Lois said, hugging a book to her tummy, "is what happened to bring about such a turnaround in her attitude toward Steve. The last time we talked you were pulling out your hair because she refused to believe he wasn't a convicted felon."

"I don't know what's going on with my daughter's head. I always thought it was the hormones that went amuck, but with her, it seems to be her brain cells. Until recently she was a perfectly normal young girl. Then overnight she turns into someone I don't even know."

"You've got to admit, this romance between you and Steve has taken several unexpected twists," Lois said, sounding both amused and pleased. "First off, you didn't even want to meet him, then once you did you both agreed not to see each other again. It would have ended there, if not for the flowers."

"Which didn't even come from Steve. He was just as glad to be done with me."

"That's not the way I remember it."

"I doubt I'll ever see him again," Meg said, slamming the cash drawer closed with enough force to move the register several inches.

"Now you're being ridiculous," Lois told her.

"I wouldn't blame him. No man in his right mind would want to get tangled up with Lindsey and me."

"I doubt that is true."

Lois sounded so sure of herself. Meg desperately wanted to believe her, but she knew better. By the time she'd closed the shop and she hadn't heard from Steve, Meg was convinced he was glad to be free of her.

Lindsey was sitting in the living room reading when Meg arrived home from work. "Hi," she said, and took a huge bite out of a big red delicious apple.

Meg set aside her purse and slipped off her shoes. The tiles in the entryway felt cool against her aching feet.

"You're not still mad at me, are you?" Lindsey asked. She leapt off the sofa and moved into the kitchen where Meg was pouring herself a cup of iced tea.

"You embarrassed me beyond belief."

"Steve wasn't embarrassed," Lindsey protested. "I just don't understand why you're so upset."

"How would you feel if I called up Dale Kotz and told him you wanted to go to the ninth-grade dance with him? He'd probably go with you, because Dale's sort of sweet on you, and we both know it. But you'd never know if Dale would have asked you himself. You'd never have the thrill of him calling you and asking you."

"Oh." Lindsey didn't say anything for several minutes.

"But it's more than that, Lindsey. I was mortified to the very marrow of my bones. I felt like you pressured Steve into proposing."

Lindsey sat in one of the kitchen chairs and hung her head. "Would it help if I told you I was sorry?"

"Yes, but it doesn't change what happened."

"You're still angry, aren't you?"

"No," Meg said, opening the refrigerator and taking out a head of lettuce for a salad. "I'm not angry any more, just incredibly embarrassed and hurt."

"I didn't mean to hurt you, Mom," Lindsey said contritely. "I was only trying to help."

"I know, honey, but you didn't. Everything is much, much worse."

Lindsey hung her head. "I feel just awful."

Meg didn't feel much better herself. She sat down at the table, next to her daughter, and patted Lindsey's hand. "It'll all come out in the wash."

Lindsey managed a weak smile, then moved into her mother's arms and buried her face in Meg's shoulder. "Men are so dumb sometimes. Love and marriage is like playing a game of connect the dots. Only with men, you have to make the dots and then draw the lines. They just don't get it."

Meg brushed the hair from her daughter's face.

"Do you love him, Mom?"

Meg smiled for the first time that day. "Yeah, I suspect I do. I certainly didn't plan on falling in love with him, that's for sure. It just sort of happened."

"I don't think he expected to fall in love with you, either."

The doorbell chimed, and horrified that she might be caught crying, Lindsey broke away from her mother and hurriedly brushed the moisture away from her face.

"I'll get it," Meg assured her. She padded barefoot into the room and opened the door.

Steve stood on the other side, holding a dozen long-stemmed roses in his hands. He smiled when she appeared. "Hello," he said, and handed her the flowers. "I thought we'd try this marriage-proposal business again, only this time we'll do it my way."

9

"Marriage proposal?" Meg repeated, staring down at the long-stemmed roses in her arms. "I'm sure you're mistaken.... Really, Steve, there's no need to do this." Her throat was already closing up on her and she could barely meet his eyes. It was worse than she'd thought it would be.

"I know exactly what I'm doing," Steve argued.

"Is it Brenda?" Lindsey whispered fiercely from the kitchen.

"No, it's Steve."

"Steve," Lindsey cried excitedly. "This is great. Maybe I didn't ruin everything after all."

"Hello, Meg," Steve said softly.

"Hi." She couldn't bring herself to look him in the eye.

"I'd like to talk to you, if that'd be all right."

"I...I was hoping we could do that," Meg told him. She handed Lindsey the flowers. "They're lovely, thank you." If she didn't hurry and say what had to be said, her throat was going to close up on her.

"Would you take care of these for me?" she asked her daughter. "Steve and I are going to talk and we'd appreciate some privacy. Okay?"

"Sure, Mom."

Lindsey disappeared into the kitchen and Meg sat down in the living room. Steve took the seat next to her and claimed her hand with his. She wished he wasn't so close. The man had a way of muddling her most organized thoughts.

"Before you say anything, I have a couple of things I'd like to talk to you about." She dragged her hand from his and cupped her knees. "I've been doing a lot of thinking and...and basically I've come to a few conclusions."

"About what?"

"Us," she said, and dragging in a deep breath she continued. "Lois reminded me this afternoon about the unexpected twists and turns our relationship has taken. First off, neither one of us wanted to meet the other—we were basically thrown into an impossible situation.

"We wouldn't have continued seeing each other if it hadn't been for the flowers your sister sent to me. From the moment we met, we've had two other people dictating our lives."

"To some extent that's true," Steve agreed, "but we wouldn't have allowed any of this to happen if we hadn't been attracted to each other from the beginning."

"Maybe," she admitted slowly.

"What do you mean, maybe?" Steve asked.

"I think that what we both need now is time apart to sort through what's happened and decide what it is we really want."

"Like hell," he argued. "I've had thirty-five years looking for what I want and I've found it. I want to make you and Lindsey a permanent part of my life."

"Ah, yes. Lindsey," Meg said, exhaling sharply. "As you might have noticed she's fifteen, going on thirty, and a handful. I have the feeling this is what the rest of the teen years are going to be like."

"So you could use a gentle hand helping you steer her in the right direction." Steve leapt to his feet and jerked his fingers through his hair. "Listen, if you're trying to tell me you'd rather I didn't propose, then just say so. I'd rather have you tell me what's on your mind than have you beat around the bush."

Meg straightened, keeping her back ramrod straight. Her vocal chords felt gnarled with emotion, and for a moment she couldn't speak. "That's what I'm saying."

Steve froze, and it was clear to Meg that he was stunned. "I see," he said after a long pregnant pause. "Then, what is it you want from me?"

Meg closed her eyes. "Maybe it'd be best if we..."

"Don't say it, Meg," he warned in low tones, "because we'll both know it's a lie."

"Maybe it'd be best if we..." she started again, feeling the necessity to say the words "...didn't see each other for a while."

Steve's smile was filled with sarcasm. "Let me tell you something, Meg Remington, because it's clear someone needs to say it. Your husband walked out on you and your daughter. It happens. It wasn't the first time a man deserted his family for another woman and it won't be the last. For the past ten years you've done one hell of a job building a concrete fence around you and Lindsey.

"No one else was allowed in until Lindsey took matters into her own hands. Now that I'm here, you don't know what to do. You started to care for me, really care, and now you're scared to death."

"Steve . . ."

"Your safe, secure world is about to be threatened by another man. Do you think I don't know you love me?" he demanded. "You're crazy about me. Hell, I feel the same way about you, and to be fair, you've done a damned good job shaking up my world, as well.

"If you want it to end here and now, then fine, but be honest about it. Be fair. You're doing it because you're afraid of knocking down those walls of yours. You're afraid to trust another man with your heart, for fear he'll walk all over you and then leave."

"You seem to have me all figured out," she managed to say, speaking around the emotion clogging her throat.

"You want me to leave without giving you this diamond burning a hole in my pocket, then fine. You got it. But don't think it's over, because it isn't. I don't give up that easy." He stalked out of the room and paused at her front door. "Don't get a false sense of security. I'll be back and next time I'm bringing reinforcements." The door closed with a bang.

"Mom," Lindsey asked, slipping into the room and sitting down next to Meg, "what happened?"

Meg struggled not to weep. "I . . . got cold feet."

"But you told me you were in love with Steve."

"I am," she whispered.

"Then why'd you send him away?"

Meg released her breath in a long, slow exercise. "Because I'm an idiot."

"Then stop him," Lindsey said urgently.

"I can't. . . . It's too late."

"No, it isn't," Lindsey argued and rushed out the front door. A part of Meg wanted to stop her daughter. Meg's pride had taken enough of a beating in the past couple of days. But her heart, her treacherous heart, knew that the battle had already been lost. She was in love with Steve Conlan.

A minute later Lindsey burst into the house, breathing hard. Panting, she pressed her hand over her heart and said between giant gulps of air, "Steve says . . . if you want to talk to him . . . you're going to have to come outside . . . yourself."

Meg clenched her hands together. "Where is he?"

"Sitting in his truck. Hurry, Mom, I don't think . . . he'll wait much longer."

With her heart pounding in her throat, Meg walked onto the porch and leaned against the support column. Steve's truck was parked at the curb.

He turned his head when he saw her. His eyes were dark and cold. Unfriendly. Unwelcoming.

Meg bit into her lip and squarely met his gaze. It demanded every ounce of resolve she possessed to step off the porch and take a few short steps toward him. She paused halfway across the freshly mowed lawn.

Steve rolled down the window. "What?" he demanded.

She blinked, her heart racing like a runaway locomotive.

"Lindsey claimed you had something you wanted to say," he said gruffly.

Meg should have known better than to let Lindsey do her talking for her. She opened her mouth but her throat muscles froze on her. Tears burned for release but she refused to cry in front of him.

"Say it!" he demanded.

"I . . . don't know that I can."

"Either you say it or I'm leaving." He twisted away from her and started the engine.

"Mom, we're going to lose him," Lindsey cried from the porch. "Don't let him go. . . . He's the best chance we've got."

"I . . . love you," she whispered.

Steve turned off the truck. "Did you say something?"

"I love you, Steve Conlan. I'm frightened out of my wits. You're right—I have built a concrete wall around my heart. I don't want to lose you. . . . It's just that I'm afraid." Her voice caught on the last word.

His eyes held hers and Meg realized he had soaked up the words like a thirsty sponge.

After a moment, Steve smiled. "That wasn't so difficult now, was it?"

"Yes, it was," she countered. "It was damn hard." He didn't seem to understand that she was standing on her front lawn with half the neighborhood looking on, while she told him how much she loved him.

"You're going to marry me, Meg Remington."

She sniffled and nodded. "Probably."

He leapt out of his truck, slammed the door and with three power-filled strides eliminated the distance between them. "Will you or will you not marry me?"

"I will," she said, laughing and crying at the same time, then she ran to meet him halfway.

"That's what I thought." Steve impatiently hauled her into his arms and buried her in his embrace. He grabbed her about the waist and whirled her around, then half carried her back into the house.

Once inside, he closed the door with his foot and pinned her against the frame, crushing her mouth with his.

The kiss was wet and wild.

Lindsey cleared her throat behind them. "I hate to interrupt, but I have a few important questions one or both of you need to answer."

Steve buried his face in Meg's neck and mumbled something Meg couldn't hear, which was probably for the best.

"Okay, kiddo, what do you want to know?" Steve asked when he'd regrouped.

"We're getting married?" Lindsey asked, and Meg was pleased the way she'd included herself.

"Yup," Steve assured her. "We're going to be a family."

Lindsey let out a holler that could be heard for three blocks.

"Where will we live? Your house or ours?"

Steve looked to Meg. "Do you care?"

She shook her head.

"We'll live wherever you want," Steve told the teenager. "I imagine staying close to your friends is important, so we'll take that into consideration."

"Great." Lindsey beamed him a smile. "What about adding to the family? Mom's willing, I think."

Once more Steve looked to Meg, and laughing, she nodded. "Oh, yes. There will be several additions to this family."

Steve's eyes grew dark and intense and Meg knew he was thinking about the same thing she was. She wanted his babies as much as she wanted this man. Just looking at him caused a soft, prickling feeling deep inside her. She had no name for this feeling other than desire for all they could discover together, all they could learn and teach each other.

"One last thing," Lindsey said.

It was hard to pull her eyes away from Steve's, but it was important to include Lindsey in their decision making. "Yes, honey."

"It's just that I'd rather you didn't go shopping for your wedding dress alone. You're really good at a lot of things, but frankly, Mom, you don't have a whole lot of fashion sense."

As it turned out, Lindsey, Brenda and Steve's sister, Nancy, were all involved in the decision-making process when it came to the all-important wedding dress. Steve, naturally, wasn't allowed within a hundred feet of Meg and the wedding dress until the day of the ceremony.

The wedding took place three months later, with family and friends gathered around them. Lindsey proudly served as her mother's maid of honor.

Steve endured all the formality because he knew it was important to Meg and Lindsey. His own mother and Nancy seemed to enjoy making plans for the wedding, as well. All that was required of him was to show up and say "I do," which suited Steve just fine.

All this fuss over the wedding was for women. Men, Steve speculated, considered it a necessary evil. Or so he believed until his wedding day. Then he saw Meg walk down the center of the church aisle. The emotion that clogged his chest came as a complete and utter surprise.

He'd known he loved her—he must have, to put up with all the craziness that had befallen their courtship. But he hadn't a clue of how deeply those tentacles had wrapped themselves around his heart. Not until he saw Meg so solemn and so damned beautiful. She stole his breath away, walking down the aisle.

The reception was a blur. Every time he looked at Meg he found it difficult to believe that this beautiful, vibrant woman was his wife. His thoughts were a jumbled, confused mess as he greeted those he needed to greet and thanked those he needed to thank.

It seemed half a lifetime before he was allowed to be alone with his wife. He'd booked the honeymoon suite at a hotel close to Sea-Tac airport. The following morning they were flying to Hawaii for two weeks. Meg had never seen the islands. Steve strongly suspected he didn't need a tropical playground to discover paradise. He would find that in her arms.

"Husband." Meg said the word shyly while Steve fumbled with the key to unlock their hotel suite. "I like the way the word sounds."

"So do I, but not quite as well as I like the sound of wife." With the door open, he swept Meg into his arms and carried her into the room.

He hadn't taken two steps before they started to kiss. Steve had thought to go about the lovemaking in a relaxed, natural way that would put her at ease.

A kiss wouldn't hurt. It was expected of him. Meg tasted of wedding cake and champagne, of passion and love. She wound her arms around his neck and enticed his tongue to explore her mouth. Steve didn't need much of an invitation.

His tongue stroked and teased until they were both panting and weak. With effort that would have left a strong man trembling and helpless, he broke off the kiss.

"We could order dinner from room service," he suggested with no real enthusiasm. The only thing he was hungry for was his wife.

"We could do that," she agreed. Her arms remained linked around his neck. "Or we could make mad, passionate love. Which do you prefer?"

At the unbridled desire he read in her eyes, Steve moaned and carried her into the center of the room. After he'd set her feet on the floor, he kissed her again slowly with all the pent-up desire stored in his head.

"Which one do you think I'd rather do?" he asked and reached behind her for the zipper of her dress. "I haven't made any secret of how much I've wanted to make love to you."

"That's true," she whispered, kissing the underside of his jaw. "I've always known exactly how hard waiting has been on you. Most men would never have held out this long."

"Most men don't have stepdaughters like Lindsey. We struck an agreement."

"Trust me, I know all about your agreement. It was very sweet of you to promise not to make love to me until after we were married, if she'd agree to remain a virgin until her wedding night."

The metal teeth rasped as he peeled open the dress. "Do you think she'll hold up her part of the bargain?"

"Who's to know...? I'd like to think so, but then, I'm her mother."

Steve peeled the fabric of her dress over one tantalizing shoulder and then the other shoulder, until it fell loosely to the floor. What was left was his wife. His wife—Steve couldn't get used to believing it was true—standing before him in nothing but the skimpiest display of silky underwear. His heart stopped entirely before it sprang back to life.

He wanted to tell her how beautiful he found her, how alluring and breathtaking, but all that he was able to manage was a weak groan.

He kissed the ivory perfection of one shoulder. Then he kissed the other, his lips blazing a trail up the side of his neck to the sweet hollow of her throat.

"You make my knees weak," she murmured.

"Mine, too."

Together they collapsed on the edge of the bed. Steve kissed her and loosened his tie. With their lips

joined, Meg's fingers worked at his shirt fastening
undressing him. His own hands were busy freeing he
from those minute slips of silk. Meg was having fa
more success than he had. He shucked off his shirt an
tie long before he managed to remove a single item
from her.

Her lacy bra was the first to go. He filled his han
with one plump breast, then he filled his mouth. H
took her nipple between his lips, savoring it with h
tongue, then tugging and teasing it until she whim
pered and rubbed her fingers in his hair.

Knowing he wouldn't last more than a minute if h
didn't pace himself, Steve broke away and discarde
the remainder of his clothing.

Meg laid back on the bed watching him, grinning
sweetly. Her gaze centered on his bulging manhood.

"Something amuses you?" he asked, kneeling ove
her. He planted his hands on either side of her face.

"You amaze me, husband."

"My reputation must precede me," he teased, kiss
ing her. "We haven't even made love yet, and alread
you're touting my powers."

"I think I'll die if you don't make love to me soon,"
she whispered, the teasing and the laughter draining
out of her eyes.

Steve shared her sentiments. He trembled with a
profound need. His hands shook as he tugged at the
waistband of her silk-and-lace bikini panties.

He had planned to wait, to talk her through their
first time together, offer reassurances, comfort her
with his love, take her in his arms.

That all changed the instant her legs were free of the restraining lace. She smiled up at him, a soft, womanly smile, and arched her hips upward in silent entreaty, in silent invitation.

"Oh, baby," he whispered.

"I need you so much."

Gritting his teeth, swallowing a moan, he positioned himself above her and slid between her legs.

Meg slowly closed her eyes and cried a soft, welcoming moan. She stretched her arms out at her sides and her fingers clenched the sheets.

Steve released a low, guttural cry at the shaft of hot desire that surged through him. He dared not move.

Meg shifted her hips and swallowed him completely.

Together they discovered an immediate rhythm. Her bare breasts and belly mated with his. He wasn't going to last much longer—not with her this hot, this tight. He tried to maintain the current pace and hold back his release by lifting her legs and looping them around his middle.

It might have worked if Meg hadn't reached her own completion. She gasped, cried out and tossed her head from side to side. Before another moment passed, Steve had joined her in a sensual oblivion that carried them straight through the gates of paradise.

Together they died. Together they were reborn.

Breathing deep and hard, Steve knew he should move off her. He was too heavy for Meg, but he couldn't make himself pull away from her. Not yet. Not so soon.

When he could, he looked down on the face of this woman he loved more than he had thought it was possible to love anything or anyone. She smiled up at him.

"Thank you," she whispered.

"I should be the one thanking you."

"But you taught me something.... You made me feel beautiful and desirable."

"You are. Every delectable inch of you."

"To you," she whispered and bit into his shoulder. She lifted her head from the mattress and lovingly pressed her mouth to his. Her kiss was long and sweet, relaxed.

Steve readjusted their bodies, afraid his weight would be too much for her. He positioned them so they lay side by side, still joined, his leg looped over her hip.

"Comfortable?" he asked.

She smiled and sighed. "Very."

He kissed her again and the magic rekindled. Steve could feel the heat curl in his belly and build in his loins.

Meg's round eyes met his and she laughed sexily. "You are an amazing husband."

"What did I tell you!"

Lindsey sat at the table with Steve's sister, Nancy, and licked the icing off her fingertips. "Do you think they'll ever figure it out?"

Nancy sipped champagne from a crystal flute. "I doubt that either one of them is thinking about much right now except each other."

"We made some real mistakes, though."

"We?" Nancy said, eyeing Lindsey.

"All right, I'll admit I nearly ruined everything by pushing the marriage issue. How was I to know my mother would take that so personally? Geez, she about had a heart attack, and all because I suggested Steve marry her."

"It all worked out, though," Nancy said, looking pleased with herself. "And heaven knows I made a few blunders of my own. Having my friend stop off at the shop and say she was Meg wasn't the smartest thing I've ever done. Steve was bound to learn sooner or later that it wasn't really Meg."

"But we had to do something," Lindsey insisted. "They were both acting like spoiled children. One of them had to give in. Besides, your ploy worked."

"Better than the flowers I sent."

Lindsey sampled another bite of wedding cake. "You know what the hardest part of all this was?"

"I know what it was for me. I had one heck of a time keeping a straight face when your mother came to the house dressed in a Tina Turner wig and five-inch heels. Oh, Lindsey, if you could have seen her."

"Steve was something of a comic himself, with his leather jacket and his bad-boy smirk."

"Neither one of them is any good at acting," Nancy said, grinning still.

"Not like us."

"Not like us," Nancy agreed.

* * * * *

Sneak Previews of September titles, from *Yours Truly*™:

MALE FOR SALE
by Tiffany White

Noelle's dateless for her *younger* sister's wedding, so she secretly buys a suit-and-tie hunk at a bachelor auction—or so she thinks. But the man she's bringing to the wedding—to meet her entire family—is the *wrong* one!

NOT LOOKING FOR A TEXAS MAN
by Lass Small

Maggie's driving down the road in a major blizzard, when suddenly, *Boom!*—a fender bender. Mr. Tall, Dark and Apologetic carries her into his warm, cozy truck until help arrives. But twenty-four hours later, she's still there—and has gotten to know him *very* well.

Available this month, from *Yours Truly*™:

WANTED: PERFECT PARTNER
by Debbie Macomber

LISTEN UP, LOVER
by Lori Herter

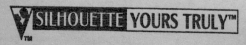

Silhouette

SPECIAL EDITION ®

™

It's our 1000th Special Edition and we're celebrating!

Join us these coming months for some wonderful stories in a special celebration of our 1000th book with some of your favorite authors!

Diana Palmer   **Nora Roberts**
Debbie Macomber   **Christine Flynn**
Phyllis Halldorson   **Lisa Jackson**

mini-series by:

Lindsay McKenna, Marie Ferrarella, Sherryl Woods, Gina Ferris Wilkins.

And many more books by special writers.

And as a special bonus, all Silhouette Special Edition titles published during Celebration 1000! Will have **double** Pages & Privileges proofs of purchase!

Silhouette Special Edition...heartwarming stories packed with emotion, just for you! You'll fall in love with our next 1000 special stories!

Love—when you least expect it!

▼ SILHOUETTE YOURS TRULY™

With the purchase of WANTED: PERFECT PARTNER
or LISTEN UP, LOVER, you can send in for a FREE
personal organizer! Perfect for your hustle-'n'-bustle
life-style.

On the proof-of-purchase coupon below, fill in your
name, address and zip or postal code, and send it, plus
$2.95 U.S. /$3.50 CAN. for postage and handling (check
or money order—please do not send cash) payable to
Silhouette Books, to: In the U.S.: 3010 Walden Avenue,
P.O. Box 9057, Buffalo, NY, 14269-9057; In Canada:
P.O. Box 622, Fort Erie, Ontario, L2A 5X3. Please allow
4-6 weeks for delivery. Order your FREE personal
organizer now; quantities are limited. Offer expires
December 31, 1995.